While We Waited

D.E. Haggerty

Copyright © 2025 D.E. Haggerty

All rights reserved.

D.E. Haggerty asserts the moral right to be identified as the author of this work.

ISBN: 9789083465524

While We Waited is a work of fiction. The names, characters, places, and incidents portrayed in it are the product of the author's imagination. Any resemblance to actual persons, living or dead, events or locations is entirely coincidental.

All rights reserved. No part of this publication may be reproduced, stored in a retrieval system, or transmitted, in any form or by any means, electronic, mechanical, photocopying, recording or otherwise, without the prior permission of the author.

No portion of this book may be reproduced in any form without written permission from the publisher or author, except as permitted by U.S. copyright law.

Also by D.E. Haggerty

Before It Was Love
After The Vows
How to Date a Rockstar
How to Love a Rockstar
How to Fall For a Rockstar
How to Be a Rockstar's Girlfriend
How to Catch a Rockstar
My Forever Love
Forever For You
Just For Forever
Stay For Forever
Only Forever
Meet Disaster
Meet Not
Meet Dare
Meet Hate
Bragg's Truth
Bragg's Love
Perfect Bragg
Bragg's Match

Bragg's Christmas
A Hero for Hailey
A Protector for Phoebe
A Soldier for Suzie
A Fox for Faith
A Christmas for Chrissie
A Valentine for Valerie
A Love for Lexi
About Face
At Arm's Length
Hands Off
Knee Deep
Molly's Misadventures

Chapter 1

Nova – a woman who hates to be told no – especially by a grumpy resort owner

NOVA

I enter *Five Fathoms Brewing* – the brewery I own with the four best friends in the world – and smile at Chloe.

"Good morning, Chloe. It's a beautiful day, isn't it? The sunrise was magnificent."

She grunts. "Sunrise? Who gets up early enough to watch the sun rise?"

Speaking of how early it is. "What are you doing here already?"

Chloe is one of the co-owners of the brewery. She's the hospitality manager for the bar and restaurant. She usually doesn't arrive at work until it's time to open the restaurant for lunch.

She motions to the broom. "What does it look like I'm doing?"

"Having a mental breakdown since you don't clean."

"I clean."

I giggle. "Do you not remember the time you rang me for help because suds were coming out of your dishwasher?"

She rolls her eyes. "That happened years ago."

"What about last month when you spilled purple laundry detergent all over your white kitchen counter and wanted to know how to dye the entire counter purple to match?"

"Purple kitchen counters are cool."

The door bangs open and two more co-owners of the brewery, Sophia and Maya, enter. "Good morning."

"Where's the coffee?" Sophia grumbles.

Chloe points to the bar. "There's a full pot."

Sophia stumbles to the bar and pours herself a cup. She downs half of it before sighing. Her brow wrinkles. "What is Chloe doing here?"

"Ahem." Chloe clears her throat. "I work here, remember?"

"But usually you don't arrive before eleven," Sophia points out.

Maya claps her hands. "Maybe it's because she got up early with her husband."

Chloe glares at Maya. "Lucas is my fake husband."

Chloe married the sexy cop next door to help him keep custody of his daughter. We're all hoping Lucas can't resist our beautiful friend. She deserves a sexy husband who can't keep his hands off of her after the way her own mother treated her.

Maya winks. "Sure, he is."

"Whatever." Chloe whirls around and stomps toward the hallway. "I've got inventory to do."

"And I've got beer to sell," I say as I make my way up the stairs to where our offices are.

I'm the sales manager for *Five Fathoms Brewing*. It's an easy job since our beer is fantastic thanks to the fifth owner, Paisley. She's always experimenting with flavors that sound as if they shouldn't go together but end up tasting awesome combined.

Sophia, Maya, and I get settled at our desks in our shared office.

"How was your evening?" Maya asks Sophia while she waits for her computer to wake up. "You seem tired. Too much fun with Flynn?" She waggles her eyebrows.

Flynn is Sophia's boyfriend. They've been obsessed with each other since high school but only recently got together. I'm surprised he hasn't asked her to marry him yet.

I sigh. Everyone's pairing off. Sophia with Flynn. Chloe with Lucas – although their relationship is supposedly 'fake'.

I want someone to love and have tons of babies with. I want a family. Someone to cuddle under the blankets with while watching movies in the evening. Someone to eat pancakes with on Sunday morning. Someone to observe the stars with at night.

I've got Finn Fable, my cat, but he's not allowed outside at night anymore. Not after he attacked the dog next door. I swear the dog was asking for it. Why else would my five-pound kitty go after a seventy-five-pound German Shepherd?

Paisley strolls into the office and stops in front of my desk. I grin up at her. "Good morning, Paisley."

"Have you spoken to Hudson yet?"

I groan. Hudson is the bane of my existence. He's also the owner of the largest resort on the island of Smuggler's Hideaway where we live. *Hideaway Haven Resort* is an exclusive hotel. It's also the only hospitality establishment on the island that doesn't serve *Five Fathoms Brewing*.

"I've spoken to Hudson numerous times," I hedge.

"She means since high school when you tried to get his attention by trying out to become a cheerleader," Sophia says.

"I didn't try out to be a cheerleader because of Hudson," I lie. "The lead cheerleader asked me to try out."

"Because she…" Maya's eyes widen and she slams a hand over her mouth. "Never mind."

"It's okay, Maya. You can say it."

Her cheeks darken and she drops her chin to stare at her fingernails. "Sorry, Nova. I didn't mean to bring her up," she whispers.

"You can talk about my mom. I won't burst into flames at the mention of her name."

My chest feels tight and my limbs heavy at the mention of Mom but I fight through the sadness. Mom's been gone for more than a decade. I'm used to the sensation by now.

Paisley's brow furrows. "Burst into flames? Why would you burst into flames?"

"Vampires burst into flames when they're exposed to sunshine. Unless they are mated to a human," Maya explains.

Sophia giggles. "Are you reading a vampire romance?"

Maya is a hopeless romantic who would rather read than deal with the world. She's lucky her job as our financial manager doesn't require her to speak to other people much. She'll literally send fifty emails to remind a customer to pay their bill rather than picking up the phone and carrying out a five-minute conversation.

She sighs. "Vampire romances are hot."

"Yes, I imagine they are if they're bursting into flames," Paisley says.

I giggle. Paisley doesn't joke often. She's usually too busy reciting random factoids. She's the smartest person I know. She can quote facts about nearly everything. Except mermaids. She doesn't believe in those. Which is a sin if you live on Smuggler's Hideaway.

She clears her throat. "Anyway, Hudson?"

"I'll contact him today."

"Tell him I have a bunch of ideas for exclusive beers at his resort."

"Hold on," Sophia says. "You do?"

Paisley pushes her glasses up her nose. "I do."

"Why didn't you tell me? Exclusive beers make for great marketing material."

Sophia is the marketing manager of *Five Fathoms Brewing*. She used to work for some hot shot marketing company in Atlanta but she came home a few months ago after she quit her job. It killed her pride to come home, but I'm glad she's back on the island. Considering she's living with the man she's been in love with forever, she's happy now as well.

"These beers will be exclusive to *Hideaway Haven Resort*," Paisley explains.

Sophia rubs her hands together. "We could do a joint marketing campaign. I love this idea. Does anyone know who the marketing manager at the resort is? Never mind. I'll figure it out." She digs her phone out of her pocket.

"Hold on," I say before she can dial. "*Hideaway Haven Resort* isn't a client."

"Yet." Sophia waves at me. "Use some of your sunshine magic on Hudson and he'll be a client in no time."

I cock an eyebrow. "My sunshine magic?"

"Oh, please. Don't act confused. You can sell fish to a mermaid."

Usually, I agree with Sophia. I am a pretty darn good salesperson. But Hudson isn't interested in my sales pitch. I can barely get him to speak to me on the phone. Let alone buy our beer.

"Please," Maya begs. "*Hideaway Haven Resort* is a huge account. Think of the financial security having the account will bring to *Five Fathoms*."

"Fine. I'll call Hudson."

I log into my computer and …

I glance up. Sophia, Maya, and Paisley are now standing in front of my desk.

"What are you doing?"

"Nothing," Sophia says at the same time Paisley says, "Eavesdropping."

I shoo them away with my hands. "I can't do a sales pitch with the three of you staring at me."

"Fine." Paisley checks her watch. "I need to get back to the brewery anyway. I have a new batch of Session IPA I'm working on."

She leaves but Sophia and Maya don't.

"I'm not calling while you stand there."

Maya shrugs. "Fine. I can hear you from my desk anyway."

Siren bait! I can't phone Hudson with them listening. My friends believe I have a thing for Hudson. I don't. Did I maybe have a teensy tiny crush on him in high school? He was the captain of the football team. Of course, I did. Every girl in school did.

But Hudson, the charming football player, is no more. He's a grump who thinks it's okay to tell women what to wear. Jerk.

I grab my phone and make my way to the bathroom. I lock the door behind me and dial Hudson's number.

"What?"

I ignore his Holy Grumpiness. "Hi, Hudson. It's Nova from *Five Fathoms Brewing*."

"What do you want?"

"I want to discuss the possibility of *Hideaway Haven Resort* carrying *Five Fathoms Brewing* beer. As you—"

"No."

I open my mouth to try again but he hangs up. Captain Cranky strikes again.

He has another thing coming if he thinks I'm giving up. I'm not.

I'll think of another approach. One he won't see coming.

Chapter 2

Hudson – the king of grumps who doesn't think he deserves sunshine

HUDSON

Damnit. I shove my phone in my pocket. I hate hanging up on Nova. But it's for the best. She's sunshine and happiness and all things good. I don't deserve good things.

There's a knock on my door. "Boss."

Great. A distraction. "What is it?"

The door opens and my front desk manager, Wesley, sticks his head inside. "Someone's asking to see the owner."

I push to my feet. My right ankle wobbles but I ignore it. I'm used to ignoring the pain.

"What's the problem?" I ask as we walk toward the lobby.

"Noise complaint."

Noise complaint? Noise complaints are extremely rare at the resort. This isn't some old hotel building with paper-thin walls. I had the place built from the ground up and made sure all the rooms are soundproof. I spent a decade of my life living in hotel rooms when I played ball in the NFL. I know how important a quiet room is.

We enter the lobby and two women come rushing toward us. Wesley clears his throat. "This is the boss, Mr. Clark."

The first woman rakes her gaze over me and licks her lips. "Oh, we know who Hudson Clark is."

Great. A football groupie. I haven't played football in three years due to my injury but groupies don't care. They throw themselves at me whether I want them to or not. It's why I returned to the island of Smuggler's Hideaway where I grew up. The locals know me and know to leave me alone.

The second woman scoots closer to stand next to her friend. "We can show you a good time, Double Crown."

I scowl. I hate the nickname Double Crown. It's pretentious. I'm not some pompous ass. Football is a team sport. I didn't win those two Super Bowls. My team did.

I cross my arms over my chest and glare at the women. "I understand there was a noise complaint."

The first woman rolls her eyes. "How else could we get your attention?"

"Yeah." The other woman nods. "We've been here all weekend and we didn't bump into you once."

Another reason I stay as far away from the guests as possible. I don't want to be the notch on some football groupie's bedpost. There's only one woman I want to spend any time in bed with. I clear my throat and force thoughts of Nova's smile out of my mind. The woman is not for me.

My cock twitches. It obviously disagrees.

"If there's no noise complaint, I need to return to my work."

I try to walk away but the first woman latches onto my bicep. "Don't go. We haven't had a chance to get to know you yet."

These women don't want to get to know me. They want to brag to their friends about how they had sex with a football player. I could be a faceless man for all they care.

The lobby doors open and two men rush inside. "Get your hands off of her!"

I raise my arms in the air. "Not touching her."

One of the men grabs the second woman and pulls her away while the other man squares up with me.

"I said. Get your hands off of my wife."

Fucking hell. I wish I could say this is the first time I've dealt with an angry husband, but it's not. It's not the second, either. I stopped counting a while ago.

"Sir, I'm not touching your wife." I wiggle my hands which are still in the air.

"I don't care how you're some big football legend. You can't go around seducing married women."

I don't seduce women period. Not since my rookie year when I caught a woman poking holes in a condom. I learned my lesson awful quick. No strange women in my hotel room.

"Sir. I'm not touching your wife," I repeat.

He yanks his wife away from me. "Not anymore you aren't."

His wife rubs her arm where he touched her. "Maybe you should focus more on how you touch your wife rather than how strangers do."

He stomps toward me and gets in my face. Never mind how at six-foot-three I'm several inches taller than him.

He pokes me in the chest. "You do not tell me how to treat my wife."

The lobby doors open again and two police officers stroll inside. I don't know who contacted them but I'm grateful they did. I have no intention of spending my Monday morning fighting with some man who doesn't know how to treat his wife.

"Well, well, well, what is Huddy up to now?"

I grit my teeth. I hate the nickname Huddy more than Double Crown. But the inhabitants of the island enjoy reminding me of how I'm plain 'ol Huddy to them.

"Hey, Weston," I greet. I went to high school with Weston. He was two grades ahead of me but in a small community like Smuggler's Hideaway, everyone knows everyone.

"Lucas," I nod to his partner who I met when he had his wedding at the resort two months ago.

Weston scans the scene and smirks. "Nothing's changed since high school I see."

"Of course, you have the police in your pocket," the husband mutters before poking me in the chest again. "This man was assaulting my wife."

"No, he wasn't," Wesley says. He sweeps an arm over the lobby where numerous people have their phones out recording the incident. Great. Just great. Those videos will be on social media within the hour. My agent is going to lose his mind.

"Everyone here knows the truth," he continues.

"And the truth is?" Lucas asks.

"Perhaps we should continue this someplace more private," I suggest.

"Private?" The husband scoffs. "You want to run away, Mr. Hot Shot Football Star?"

"I was trying to save you from embarrassment but if you want to do this here, fine by me." I shrug. It won't be the first time my face is on the front page of a gossip magazine. I would hope it'll be the last, but I know better.

"Save me from embarrassment?" he shouts. "You're the one who tried to steal my wife away."

Steal his wife away? Really? I met her less than five minutes ago.

"And you're the one who assaulted your wife when you grabbed her."

The atmosphere in the room becomes icy but he doesn't notice. "She's my wife. I can't assault her! She's mine!"

Weston steps in front of the man. "It's time for us to have a little chat. In private."

"This is bullshit."

Weston removes his handcuffs from his belt and twirls them in the air. "We can do this the easy way or the hard way. Your decision."

"You're protecting him because he's a football player."

"I've known Huddy since before he could throw a ball," Weston says. "If I recall correctly, he peed on the first football his dad ever gave him."

"Weston," I growl. "It's not story time."

He shrugs. "Merely showing the man how I'm not biased."

"Not biased my ass!" The man screams in Weston's face. "You're handcuffing me while he gets away with trying to steal my wife from me."

"I wasn't handcuffing you, but I am now."

Weston quickly secures the man before leading him out the door. "I'll get his statement. You get the witness statements," he instructs Lucas.

The second the door closes behind them, his wife throws herself at me. "Thank you. Thank you."

I raise my hands in the air and grit my teeth. I don't want her touching me. If any woman is going to touch me, it'll be—

I shove thoughts of Nova and her bright smile away. No women will be touching me. Period.

Lucas untangles the woman from me. "Is there somewhere we can speak privately?"

I nod to my front desk manager. "Wesley will show you the way to a private conference room you can use."

"Can you have someone round up any footage they recorded of the incident?" he asks before starting down the hallway behind Wesley.

"I'll handle it, boss," one of the front desk workers, Roger, says.

The woman's friend hurries after them. "Can I go with her? For moral support?"

Lucas agrees and the three of them disappear down the hallway with Wesley while Roger herds everyone together. He asks everyone for their name and email address before checking the footage on their phones and forwarding it to the resort. I'm impressed. I'll keep my eye on the man in the future.

Another hour passes before all the witnesses have been interviewed by Lucas and Weston. I remain in the lobby to oversee the situation in case I'm needed.

When Weston and Lucas finally depart, with the husband handcuffed in the back of their patrol car, I make my way back to my office. I shut the door behind me and collapse in my chair.

What a morning.

My phone rings and I dig it out of my pocket. *Nova calling.*

I'm tempted to answer. Just to hear her happy voice.

But I don't. I hit ignore and throw the phone on my desk.

Nova should stay far, far away from me.

Chapter 3

No – a word Nova refuses to accept when it comes to Hudson and beer

NOVA

"Hang up on me will he," I mutter as I drive to *Hideaway Haven Resort*.

I'm done with Grumbleguts and his inability to at least have a conversation about the possibility of stocking *Five Fathoms* beers at his resort. Does he think he's too special to have local beer on the menu? I'll show him special.

I arrive at the resort and park near the entrance to the hotel. I grab the bag I prepared and march to the door. It opens automatically and I hurry inside.

I glance around and nearly screech to a halt. I forgot how fancy this place is. Soaring ceilings stretch high above, a grand staircase sweeps gracefully upward in a spiral with handrails carved from rich dark wood, and a breathtaking chandelier with crystals shimmers in the light. To top it all off, the entire place is adorned with tropical blooms.

I glance down at my outfit. I'm wearing a sundress and flip-flops. Maybe *Hideaway Haven Resort* is too special to carry our beer.

A man approaches me. According to his nametag, he's Roger. "Can I help you?"

I ignore all my insecurities and smile at him. "Hi, Roger. Is Hudson available?"

His eyes narrow. "Do you have an appointment?"

I nearly roll my eyes. As if Hudson would ever agree to an appointment with me. I lie instead. "Yes, I do."

He studies me for a moment before motioning for me to follow him. "This way, please."

I walk through the lobby as if I belong there. We enter a hallway behind the reception area and continue until we reach a door marked *Hudson Clark*.

"Thank you for accompanying me," I tell him. He nods before backing away.

I wait until he's gone before I knock on the door.

"Hudson," I holler as I knock. When he doesn't respond, I open the door. Damn. His office is empty. Where is he? I can hardly go ask Roger after lying about having an appointment.

I notice a door at the end of the hallway and aim for it. It leads outside. I scan the area but there's no sign of Hudson.

Kraken's curse! Where is he?

I've come this far. I'm not giving up now. I will find Hudson and I will secure a deal with him to sell *Five Fathoms* beer at his fancy schmancy resort.

To the left is the beach. I don't bother with it. Hudson doesn't enjoy the beach. Too much sand and sun for the Grumblebee. I turn toward the chalets scattered throughout the resort instead.

I meander through the paths lined with greenery and small ponds. It's peaceful here. The entire resort vibe is the complete opposite to the rest of the island of Smuggler's Hideaway where shenanigans rule the day.

Don't get me wrong. I love shenanigans as much as the next smuggler but I could get used to the peace and quiet here.

I spot a golfcart in front of a chalet. Guessing by the tiles stacked outside, this chalet is still under construction. Excellent. I bet Hudson is here.

Holy mermaids! I nearly shout when I enter the chalet. This place is fantastic. My eye immediately catches on the wall of windows with a view of the ocean. There's also a plunge pool on the patio. I'm drawn to it. I love swimming but I hate salt water. Which sucks when you live on an island where pools are rare because you can swim in the ocean.

"What are you doing here?"

I whirl around with a hand on my chest. "You scared the kraken out of me."

Hudson crosses his arms over his chest and his biceps bulge with the action. Despite no longer being a professional athlete, he keeps in shape. There's not an ounce of fat on him. I long to touch every inch of his body to feel those muscles for myself. Are they smooth and hard?

He clears his throat and I lift my gaze to his face. He couldn't be a bit ugly? Nope. Not Hudson. Deep, dark brown eyes I could drown in. A square jaw I want to explore with my fingers. His face is perfect except for a bump on his nose from where he broke it playing college ball.

His face should adorn magazines. What am I saying? It has adorned magazines. There's a chance I have a copy of each of those magazines. But I'll never admit it out loud.

"I scared you? You're the one who's trespassing."

"I'm not trespassing. I came to speak to you."

He scowls. "I don't want to speak to you."

Don't be discouraged, Nova. Don't be discouraged.

I beam up at him. "I want to discuss the possibility of *Hideaway Haven Resort* carrying *Five Fathoms* beer."

"I told you. We already have a beer supplier."

"But don't you want to carry the local beer?"

"I'm not interested in your little hobby brewery."

Hobby brewery? Is he serious? *Five Fathoms Brewing* is stocked in grocery stores all along the Atlantic coast. We are a serious business with serious beer.

I inhale a deep breath and shove all my annoyance away.

"I'm not going anywhere until you at least try one of our beers."

"Not interested." He grunts and strolls to the front door. I rush to intercept him.

"No." I block the door. "One little itty bitty sip of a beer is all I ask."

"It won't make a difference. I'm not interested in switching suppliers."

"You don't have to switch suppliers. You can add *Five Fathoms* to your current array of beers, wines, and spirits."

He motions for me to get out of his way. "I'm a busy man. I don't have time for this."

I tilt my head and study him. "Can't you do math?"

He growls. "Being a football player doesn't make me stupid."

"I'm not saying you are. But think about it. If you try the beer and don't enjoy it, I'll stop bothering you. No more phone calls. No more surprise visits. Nova Myers will cease to exist for you."

He scowls. "This is ridiculous." He motions to the door. "Move."

"No." I slam the door shut.

"Fuck." He rubs the back of his neck.

"Don't be such a sourpuss. Try the beer." I wave my bag at him. "And you can leave."

"No, I can't."

My brow wrinkles. "What? What do you mean?"

He points to the door. "You locked us in."

"You're holding an entire ring of keys."

"Which work from the outside. The inner lock hasn't been configured yet."

"Surely, you can phone someone to open the door for us."

He wiggles his phone. "No reception here."

I dig my phone out of my bag and unlock it. "No bars."

"We're locked in until the construction crew returns."

I check the time. It's barely four. "The workday isn't done yet."

"Wrong. They needed supplies and quit early. They aren't planning to return until tomorrow."

I gulp. "Tomorrow?"

He nods. "Tomorrow."

I'm stuck in this chalet with the King of Grumps for an entire night? My body tingles. I ignore it. Hudson may be the sexiest man I've ever seen. But nothing is happening here. He doesn't want me and I don't want him.

Liar.

I ignore the little voice in the back of my mind. She's wrong. I'm not *that* desperate for a man to love. I won't throw myself at Hudson who's made it perfectly clear he doesn't want to spend any time with me.

I need a diversion. Lucky for me, I've got the perfect one in my hand.

I lift the bag I'm carrying. "Good thing I have drinks and snacks then." His stomach growls and I grin. I've got him now.

"Have a seat." I motion toward the sofa before making my way to the kitchenette. Although, referring to this area as a kitchenette is an understatement. It's nicer than my kitchen at home with its marble countertops, teak cabinets, and stainless steel appliances.

I open the first cabinet to discover it filled with crystal glasses. "Wow. I'm surprised you're not renting this chalet out yet."

Hudson reaches past me to grab two beer glasses. His scent of sandalwood envelopes me and I close my eyes to memorize it. The smell reminds me of my dad. I don't remember much about him but his scent filled the house I shared with my mom after he passed away.

"Some of the tiles broke in the bathroom. They need to be replaced."

He sets the beer glasses on the counter and steps back. With his scent no longer messing with me, I remember how to speak.

"Sucky. The summer season is nearly over."

He shrugs and I watch his shoulders move up and down. I bet they're strong enough to pick me up and set me on this counter before having his wicked way with me. My panties dampen in anticipation.

I clear my throat. There is no anticipation. No one will be having their wicked way with anyone. We're stuck here for the night is all.

Nothing more. Nothing less.

Chapter 4

Timeout – What Hudson wants to call before he gives into the temptation of Nova

Hudson

Nova bends over to open a lower cabinet and my cock twitches in response. Her ass is a sight to behold. Perfectly round. I want to dig my fingers into her hips while I bury myself deep inside of her.

I retreat a few steps before I give in to temptation and flip her dress up to discover what panties she's wearing. I bet they're cute. Everything Nova wears is adorable.

Once I've seen her panties, I'd rip them off of her to discover the treasure below. I bet she tastes fantastic.

"Aha!" Nova waves a cutting board in the air. "This will do perfectly."

She sets the board on the counter before opening her bag and bringing out bags of pretzels and chips, as well as some salami and cheese. She arranges the items on the board.

"Here. Take this into the living area while I pour our beers."

I accept the board but don't move away. Witnessing Nova fiddle around a kitchen is too intoxicating a sight to walk away from. I stare as she pops open two cans of beer and pours the contents into the beer glasses I set out for her. Once she's finished, I wave her to the living area in front of me.

We settle on the sofa and she hands me the beer. "This is our Summer IPA. It's our best seller."

I sip the beer. The flavor of hops, lavender, and something spicy hits my tongue. It's good. It's really good.

"What do you think?" Nova's smile nearly blinds me. She smiles with her entire face. Her eyes light up and sparkle, her cheeks darken, and her lips spread from ear to ear.

"It's good," I grunt. I wish I could lie and say the beer sucks – it would make my life way easier if the beer wasn't drinkable – but I can't lie to her. Not about this at least.

"Good?" She rolls her eyes. "You're practically making love to your glass. It's more than good."

I notice I'm caressing the glass. Shit. I set it down on the coffee table.

"I can taste lavender and spice. What's the spice?" I ask before she can joke any further about me stroking my glass. It wasn't the beer I was imagining making love to. But Nova doesn't need to know how often I imagine her naked while stroking myself in the shower.

"Trade secret." She winks before giggling. "I'm kidding. I don't know. It's some kind of pepper. I can ask Paisley if you want to know the exact pepper."

She digs her phone out of her bag but I stop her.

"No reception, remember?"

"I'll ask her tomorrow and let you know." She stands. "I brought a variety of beers for you to try. Let me get them."

I don't want to try the beers. I know they're good. I stick to my resort but I'm not a hermit. I've spent time at the *Bootlegger* bar in the town of Smuggler's Rest where I've tried *Five Fathoms* beer. It's the only beer they carry.

Most of the establishments on the island of Smuggler's Hideaway have exclusive agreements with *Five Fathoms Brewing*. Nova smiles at the owners and they fall at her feet. I don't blame them.

"No need. I'm not switching suppliers."

"I told you. There's no need to switch. You can add our beers as an addition to whatever you're currently carrying. I'm confident your guests will prefer our beers."

She doesn't get it. I don't want to carry *Five Fathoms* beer because I need to stay away from Nova. Ever since I returned home after my career ended with a ruptured Achilles' tendon, I've avoided her.

Nova is my personal temptation. With her long brown hair I long to fist in my hand while devouring her luscious lips. And exotic dark eyes I want to watch flare with passion whenever I touch her silky smooth skin. She's practically irresistible.

But Nova is light and sunshine. I don't want to dim her light with my grumpy ass.

She presses a can into my hands. "At least try it."

I slam the can on the table. "It doesn't matter what I think of the beer, I'm not going to sell it to my customers."

She fists her hands at her hips and her breasts jut out. Her breasts are nearly as magnificent as her ass. They're larger than average, which is fine by me since my hands are larger than average. I want to lick and suck them until she's squirming beneath me, begging me for relief.

My cock hardens and lengthens as the vision of Nova naked on my bed flitters through my mind. It's on board with this plan. It's been pushing me toward Nova since high school when the two-year age difference was insurmountable.

"Why? Why is *Five Fathoms* not good enough for you?"

I glare. "I didn't say *Five Fathoms* isn't good enough."

"Yes. You. Did. You said it doesn't matter how good it tastes, the beer isn't good enough for your hoity toity clients. Must be nice to be a famous football player who can build a big fancy resort with all of his millions."

"I'm not a football player anymore."

"You have two Super Bowl rings and a Heisman trophy, I think you're good."

"You have no idea what you're talking about," I grumble. She's living her dream – owning a business with her best friends and living on the island she loves. Whereas my dream was destroyed by a defensive lineman.

"Hey now." She wags her finger at me. "Being kicked off the cheerleading squad doesn't mean I don't understand football."

"I'm not referring to football."

"Oh right." She snaps her fingers. "You're referring to how you're a big hot shot and our little brewery isn't good enough for you."

"I didn't say you aren't good enough."

"You'd be lying if you did. *Five Fathoms* is available in grocery stores all along the East Coast. From Maine to Florida. Not such a hobby brewery anymore, are we?"

Shit. I never should have said hobby brewery. I'm an asshole. I stand and prowl toward her.

"I didn't say you aren't good enough."

She retreats until her back hits the wall. But she doesn't cower. She's not afraid of me. "And yet you won't stock our beer at your fancy resort."

I slam my hands against the wall to cage her in, and her eyes flare with passion. "Stop saying *Hideaway Haven Resort* is fancy."

She snorts. "It is fancy and we're not good enough."

"It's not a contest."

"Oh yeah?" She raises her eyebrows. "If it's not a contest, why won't you stock our beer?"

Does Nova not understand the word no? She pushes and pushes and pushes. She never gives up. Which is why I've avoided her phone calls. It's hard to say no to her.

"Because I don't want to."

"Because we're not good enough."

"Enough!" I shout. "Stop saying you're not good enough."

"We're not good enough. We're not good enough. We're not—"

Something snaps inside of me. The hold I had on my control vanishes, and I slam my lips to hers. The second I feel her soft lips, I'm lost. She moans and I shove my tongue inside her mouth. She tastes of beer and cheese and something uniquely Nova. It could easily become addictive.

She digs her fingers into my hips and I wrap my arms around her and haul her near. Once her body is pressed against mine, I push my hard cock into her stomach and she moans in response.

Fuck yeah. She wants me.

I'm probably going to regret this but I'm not stopping.

I can't.

This is Nova. My personal definition of temptation.

Chapter 5

Gameday – When Hudson gives up his control and gets back on the field

HUDSON

I pick Nova up and carry her bridal style toward the bedroom. Her lips are swollen from my kisses and her exotic eyes are wide with wonder. She's more beautiful than ever. I could stare at her for days.

My cock presses against my zipper to remind me it wants more than to merely gaze into Nova's eyes. It wants to sink into her warmth until we're both spent. My blood heats as I imagine how good she'll feel.

I enter the bedroom. Thankfully, the room is already furnished with a bed. Since this is the only time I'm going to allow myself to have Nova, I want a bed to move around in. I want her comfortable when she begs me to let her come.

I lay her on the bed and come down on top of her. I brush the hair off of her face.

"Is this okay?"

She beams at me. "More than okay."

Her smile warms me, but it may vanish once I make things clear. I don't want any misunderstandings between us.

"This is only sex. Nothing more." No matter how much I want it to be more, it can't be. Nova is too good for the likes of me.

She rolls her eyes. "I get it. You don't want anything from me but sex."

If she knew what I truly desire from her, she'd go running for the ocean. Locked doors be damned. No one wants a grump to bring them down.

"And you're okay with this?" I need to be sure. I don't want to hurt her. I never want to hurt Nova.

"Am I in this bed with you?" When I don't answer, she pokes my chest. "Answer the question."

"Sorry. I thought it was rhetorical."

"It wasn't. Am I in this bed with you?"

"Yes, you are."

"Then, I'm okay with this."

Relief mixed with a hint of disappointment rolls through me. She gets it. She's not one of those football groupies who'll make sex out to be more. Although, maybe if I pushed a bit, I could—

I shut those thoughts down. This is sex and nothing more.

Nova wiggles beneath me. "Are you going to stare at me all day or are you going to rock my world?"

I palm her neck and squeeze. "You want me to rock your world?"

"If you're up for the task."

"Oh, Sunshine, I'm up for the task."

She opens her mouth to respond but discussion time is over. I meld my lips to hers. I need more and press my tongue against her lips. She opens for me and I thrust my tongue inside. Her taste hits me and I groan before using my hold on her neck to tilt her head to my liking.

I plunder her mouth in a bid to taste every single inch. I need to memorize everything about her, everything about her little moans and gasps. This is my one chance to learn all there is about Nova and I'm not squandering it.

Her hands roam over my back. Her caresses have me dangerously close to coming in my jeans. Not acceptable.

With more control than I thought I had, I wrench my mouth from hers.

"No touching," I growl.

"But touching is the best part." She sticks out her bottom lip in a pout.

I nip her lip in punishment. "No touching."

She wraps her legs around my waist. "Is this touching?"

I grunt since I can't seem to form words any longer.

"What about this?" She rubs her core against my cock and I lose all control.

I get to my knees and unwind her legs from my waist before pinning them to the bed. Her dress is bunched up and her creamy thighs are on display. I glide my hands up and down her legs. My big hands look clumsy against her skin.

"I like this touching," she breathes out.

"How about this?"

I push her dress up further to reveal her panties. They're pink and have little hearts on them. I knew they'd be cute. Everything about this woman is absolutely adorable. Her panties are no exception.

I draw one finger down the gusset of her panties. I smirk when I feel the wet spot there. She wants me. Me, the grumpy man who hasn't been very nice to her since I returned to town three years ago.

"I want to taste you."

She shivers. "I'm not stopping you."

I draw her panties down her legs and throw them behind me. And now she's bare to me. Except for her dress hitched high beneath her breasts. But I don't have time to worry about her dress now.

I settle my shoulders between her thighs. I pull her lips apart and drag my nose along her slit as I inhale her scent. She smells of wildflowers. Appropriate, since she drives me fucking wild.

I circle her clit with my tongue and her hands thread through my hair.

I want to drive her wild. The way she drives me wild. I want her screaming my name as she comes all over my tongue.

I circle her clit again and she moans as she lifts up to shove her core into my face. It's a good start.

I continue to play with her clit until her nails are digging into my head. Once she's moaning and writhing beneath me, I thrust my tongue into her pussy.

Her thighs press against my ears as she moans, "Yes. Yes. Yes."

I pump my tongue in and out of her and her walls tighten around me. I've barely begun to taste her and she's already on the brink. I fucking love how responsive she is to me.

I pinch her clit while I sink my tongue into her and she explodes. "Holy mermaids!"

I lap up her juices until she collapses on the bed. I get to my knees.

Nova is a sight to behold. Her blush travels from her cheeks down her chest. Her brow is sweaty and her hair is sticking to it. What I wouldn't give to see her this way more often. I shove those thoughts away.

I have the object of my desires in bed with me. This is no time to get melancholy.

"The next time you come, you say my name."

Her eyes flip open. "Next time? You think you can make me come again?"

I growl. "I know I can."

She giggles. "Goodie."

I nearly chuckle. The emotion surprises me. Amusement is not an emotion I've experienced very often since coming back home.

"Raise your arms."

She doesn't hesitate to follow my orders. She's fucking perfect. For tonight, I remind myself. This is only for tonight.

I grasp the hem of her dress to pull it up and off of her revealing her naked body to me.

"You weren't wearing a bra?"

"No need. The dress has a built-in bra." She gathers her breasts in her hands. "Something wrong with me not wearing a bra?"

I bat her hands out of the way. I want to be the one touching her skin, kneading her breasts.

I glide a finger around her nipple. She moans and her eyes fall shut.

I knead and massage her breasts until she arches her back and thrusts her chest at me. Time to taste. I lick and nibble at her skin before taking her nipple into my mouth.

She wraps her legs around my waist and begins rubbing herself up and down my hard cock. Her hands clench the sheets as she writhes beneath me.

I sneak a hand between our bodies to find her clit. I rub circles around it until Nova is panting. Only then do I plunge two fingers into her pussy. Her walls immediately clench around my fingers.

"Yes!"

I pause my thrusts. "What do you say when you come?"

Her eyes fly open. "Don't stop. I'm there."

"What do you say?" I growl.

"Hudson."

I reward her with another thrust.

"Hudson!" she screams as she climaxes.

I continue to pump in and out of her until her orgasm wanes.

"That's two."

Her eyes fly open. "You're counting."

I grunt.

"Does this mean we're not finished?"

In response, I stand and rip my shirt off before pushing my jeans down my legs and kicking them off. "Not finished."

I climb onto the bed and settle between Nova's thighs. I notch my cock at her entrance and—

"Fuck."

"What's wrong?"

"No condom."

I inch away from her but she circles my waist with her legs to stop me. "I have an IUD."

If anyone other than Nova said those words, I'd call bullshit and walk away. But this is Nova. My sunshine would never lie to me.

"I'm safe."

She smiles at me and my heart skips a beat. I wish I was worthy of her smile. "I trust you. And I'm safe, too. It's been a long time since I've…" She motions between us. "You know."

"Fucked a man."

She blushes. She's naked and come twice for me already but the use of the word fuck has her blushing. It's adorable.

I hitch my cock at her entrance again. "You sure?"

"I'm sure."

I sink into her warmth and her walls cling to me. I have to grit my teeth to stop myself from coming before I'm fully seated.

I won't come before she does. I'll rock her world and give her a night to remember.

And then I'll walk away.

Because Nova is not the woman meant for me. I'm undeserving of her sunshine.

Chapter 6

Sammy – a seal that is not a traffic stop but is a great listener

NOVA

I awake surrounded by the scent of sandalwood. Did I dig one of Dad's old flannel shirts out of a box and wrap it around me again?

An arm tightens around my waist and memories of last night crash into me. Dad's old shirt is not the scent I'm smelling.

I can't believe I had sex with Hudson. A man who hates me. A man who thinks I'm not good enough for him. A man who gave me more orgasms than any other man has ever before.

Ugh. This is a disaster.

I can't wake up with Hudson and see the disgust on his face. I can handle a lot of things but the man I've crushed on since tenth grade looking at me with disgust, is not one of them.

I lift the arm from around my waist and scooch out of bed. Hudson rolls over to his other side. The sheet is wrapped around his waist allowing me a view of his back. My fingers itch to touch his skin. To feel those muscles ripple.

I fist my hands. No gawking at the man who hates me.

I throw on my sundress but my panties are nowhere to be found. Oh well. It wouldn't truly be a walk of shame with panties on anyway.

Walk of shame? I gulp. I have to walk through *Hideaway Haven Resort,* the fancy pants resort that's too good to carry *Five Fathoms* beer, in yesterday's dress with no panties on.

I tiptoe to the living room and gather my things before slipping into my flip-flops. I try the front door but it's locked.

Curse the kraken! I forgot about us being locked in. It's the reason—

Nope. No. No. No. No thinking about last night.

I spin around and scan the chalet. There must be another way to get out. I should have searched last night but I was too busy trying to sell beer to one cranky resort owner.

Good job, Nova. Mission accomplished. Not.

I hurry to the sliding doors to the deck. I pull on one and it opens. Yes! Escape is mine.

I slip out the door and pause for a moment to gaze at the plunge pool. What I wouldn't give to have a pool of my own. But not all of us have millions from being an NFL superstar.

I make my way around the chalet until I'm on the path toward the main resort building. I hurry as fast as I can considering I'm wearing flip-flops, have no panties on, and am carrying a large bag with beer and food.

"Good morning," Roger, the front desk worker, greets as he approaches me.

"Good morning," I infuse my voice with cheer I'm not feeling this morning.

"Have you seen Mr. Clark? No one's seen him since late yesterday afternoon."

Probably because he was locked in a chalet doing dirty things to me. I feel my cheeks heat but ignore them.

"Nope. I haven't seen Hudson since yesterday."

I scurry away but his voice stops me.

"Where did you see him yesterday? I can start there."

"His office," I lie.

Forget about walking. I sprint down the paths until I arrive at the parking lot. Never mind how my breasts bounce. I need to get out of here pronto.

When I arrive at my car, I throw the bag in the passenger seat and jump in. My tires squeal as I peel out of the parking lot. This is not me. I don't speed. I don't break laws of any kind. Assuming I'm alone. When I'm with my friends, all bets are off.

I turn toward the town of Smuggler's Rest and force myself to slow down. I'm not an escapee from prison. There's no reason to risk a speeding ticket. I don't want to imagine what kind of rumors would spread if a police officer pulled me over as I sped away from Hudson's resort early in the morning.

I notice the time. Uh oh. It's not as early as I thought. I'm going to be late for work and my friends will ask questions. Questions I have no intention of answering. Ever.

I push my foot down on the pedal to speed up but when I round a corner, a gray lump is blocking the middle of the street. I hurry to brake before I hit it.

I skid to a halt but the lump doesn't move. Typical.

I open my door and walk toward it. "Sammy."

The seal raises his head.

"You're not supposed to be lying in the middle of the street."

I swear Sammy raises an eyebrow.

"Yeah, yeah, I shouldn't be driving home at this hour either."

I sit down next to him. Close but not touching considering a seal is still a wild animal. I cross my legs at my ankles since I'm well aware of the lack of panties situation.

"I couldn't help myself. Have you seen Hudson?"

Sammy barks. I interpret his bark as a yes.

"Sexy, right?"

He barks again.

"I couldn't resist him." I sigh. "I've wanted him since tenth grade. Although in tenth grade I didn't know much about sex. I would have kissed him, though. Hudson's a good kisser."

This time Sammy's bark resembles a question.

"I don't know how many girls he's kissed. He was a football player. He's probably kissed thousands of girls."

Which is kind of ick now I'm thinking about it. But in the three years since Hudson's been home, I haven't seen him with a woman on his arm once. Of course, he owns a resort. He could have the pick of the female guests and no one would be the wiser.

"Nope. I don't want to think about it." I stand. "Time to get off the road, Sammy boy."

He barks.

"I don't care if the road is warm and the sun is shining on you and there's no one around, it's a road."

He covers his eyes with his fins.

"You can't ignore me." I wag a finger at him. "I'm not above calling the dogcatchers on you."

He barks again but this time he scoots off of the road. Not far. He's on the shoulder but at least he's not in the middle of the road.

I wave at him. "See ya, later, Sammy."

I switch on my car and drive away slowly. I wouldn't put it past Sammy to hobble back on the road to tease me. The seal is a menace, but he's cute.

My phone rings. "Hello."

"Are you in your car?" Sophia asks.

"Yes."

"But you can walk to the brewery from your house."

"I'm well aware of how far my house is from the brewery."

"And you're late to work."

"I'll be there soon," I say instead of confirming how late I am.

"Holy mermaids!" She squeals in excitement. "Did you go home with a man last night?"

"No." It's not a complete lie. I didn't go home with Hudson. Being locked together in a chalet is not the same thing.

"Really? Are you sure?"

"I think I'd know if I went home with a man last night." Still not a lie.

She sighs. "Why didn't you go home with a man last night?"

"You've got sex on the brain ever since you and Flynn got together."

"It's awesome." She clears her throat. "But seriously, why are you driving if you didn't get some last night?"

"There are other reasons to be in my car. I could be coming home from the doctor or the pharmacy."

"Shoot the mermaids. Are you sick? What's wrong? Do I need to bring you some of my mom's chicken noodle soup? She can have a batch ready by lunch."

My stomach gurgles as guilt slams into me. My friends are well aware of my abnormal anxiety about my health, but they don't ever call me out for it. They accept me for who I am.

And yet here I am lying to Sophia, one of my best friends in the world.

"I'm fine. I'll be in the office in half an hour." Just as soon as I shower the sex off of me and put on some clean panties.

"Why don't you stay at home and work from there? I know you prefer your own surroundings when you're not feeling well."

Tears well in my eyes. She's being super sweet and I'm lying to her. Well, not exactly lying. My tummy does feel funny. But I'm definitely withholding information from her.

I suck the tears back in. I love Sophia and my friends but they don't need to know about every time I have sex. I'm allowed a private life.

"I'll be in soon."

I want to be at the office surrounded by my friends. If I stay at home, I'll spend the entire time thinking about last night. Wondering what possessed me to have sex with Hudson when

I know he can't stand me. Wondering how sex can be fantastic with someone who doesn't have feelings for you.

"No rush," Sophia says and hangs up.

Despite her words, I rush home. Thoughts of Hudson and what we did last night are banging at my barriers. I need a distraction.

I need my friends.

What I don't need is a man who can't stand me.

Forget him. We'll make *Five Fathoms Brewing* a huge success without him.

The thought of shoving our success in his face has me snickering. I'll show him I'm good enough for him.

Chapter 7

Scrambling – When Hudson runs around trying not to obsess over his night with Nova

HUDSON

I roll over and reach for Nova but the sheets are cold to my touch. I open my eyes to discover her side of the bed is empty.

I want to jump out of the bed and chase after her, but I don't. She deserves better than a grump like me.

Wait a minute. How did she leave? We're locked in here for all she knows. I climb out of bed and don my boxer shorts before making my way to the kitchen.

"Nova!" I shout her name but there's no reply.

I feel a slight breeze and notice the sliding glass door to the patio is open. Fuck. I hope she doesn't figure out that I knew we could escape last night. She'll be thoroughly pissed at me. Assuming she isn't already pissed at me for taking advantage of her last night.

I couldn't help myself. Nova and her smile are irresistible.

I return to the bedroom and dress. I notice Nova's panties in the corner and shove them in my pocket. Then, I strip the sheets off of the bed. I'm carrying them to the patio doors when the front door opens.

"What are you doing in here?" My contractor, Flynn, asks.

I hold up the sheets. "These needed to be washed since the chalet isn't ready yet."

He cocks a brow. "And you're the one who came here to change the sheets?"

I've known Flynn most of my life. He's a few years older than me but in a place the size of Smuggler's Hideaway where everyone knows everyone, a few years don't make a difference. Since he began construction on the luxury chalets at the resort, we've become friends.

But I can't tell him about last night. Nova is friends with his girlfriend, Sophia. I don't want Nova to think I was bragging about having sex with her.

"Private," I grunt.

"And it has nothing to do with Nova tearing out of the resort parking lot?"

I scowl. Nova shouldn't be speeding. It's dangerous. Especially on Smuggler's Hideaway where seals and sheep regularly cross the road without warning.

Flynn holds up his hands. "Message received. It's not my business."

My scowl wasn't meant for him, but I use the opportunity to switch topics. "Will you finish the chalet today?"

He scratches his neck. "Today? Today is pushing it."

"This chalet was supposed to be operational at the start of the month. I've lost bookings."

He sighs. "I'm sorry. I fired the kid who dropped the wet saw on the floor."

The chalet was finished, but then one of his workers dropped a saw on the bathroom floor and cracked a bunch of floor tiles.

"If he would have told us what happened, we could have fixed it right away. But instead, he hid the problem." Flynn blows out a breath. "I hate firing young kids."

"If they can't do the job, they need to go."

"Doesn't make it any easier when you bump into the person at the grocery store."

There's an easy solution to his problem. "Don't go to the grocery store."

He chuckles. "Not all of us are multi-millionaires with a restaurant kitchen at our beck and call."

I hate discussing my wealth. I don't give a shit about the money. I'd rather be playing football. My ankle twinges to remind me of why I'm not living my dream.

"When will you finish?"

Flynn frowns as he considers my question. "Should be a couple of days. A week at most."

His vague answer is unacceptable. I can't do business with vague answers. "When can I accept bookings for the chalet?"

He clears his throat. "Next week."

I lift an eyebrow. "Next week?"

"Yes." He nods. "Next week. I'll make sure of it personally even if I have to lay the tiles and do the grouting myself."

"Thanks. I'll let my sales team know they can accept reservations for the chalet from next week onward."

I walk toward the sliding doors but Flynn clears his throat. "The front door is open now."

I don't say a word. I merely pivot and walk to the front door. I notice Flynn's smirk but I ignore it. He won't hear from me how I defiled Nova all night long. It's none of his business.

I barely make it out of the chalet before Roger rushes toward me. "There you are!"

"Here I am."

"Wesley and I have been searching for you everywhere."

This is why I rarely leave the resort. Not because I'm a hermit, but because there's always someone who needs me. Managing a resort is more work than I could have imagined.

"What's wrong?"

Roger reaches for the sheets. "Let me handle those for you."

I retreat a step. "I've got it."

His hands flutter in the air for a moment before he drops them. "Okay."

I begin marching toward the main building of the resort. "What's the issue?"

"Two drunk clients."

Drunk guests? "It's barely eight in the morning."

Alcohol is readily available in the resort. People do come here to relax after all. But drunk patrons causing issues are rare.

"They've been drinking from their minibar since the bar closed last night."

"When are they scheduled to check out?"

He consults his tablet. "In two days."

"Have their minibars emptied of all alcohol."

"They'll complain."

"They can complain to me."

"Whatever you say, boss."

We reach the building and he opens the door for me. I aim for the laundry room and deposit the sheets in the dirty laundry bin. I'm tempted to sniff them one more time to gather Nova's scent but Roger's watching me closely.

"Where are the guests?"

He motions toward the beach. "At the main outdoor pool."

I hope they aren't actually in the pool. I'm not in the mood for a swim this morning.

The main pool is accessed via the glass doors in the lobby. As I travel through the area, several people try to get my attention. I ignore them.

You'd think wealthy people would be used to meeting famous athletes. You'd be wrong. What they're used to is getting whatever they want. This is why I usually stick to my office or my chalet at the back of the property.

"It's Double Crown," a man shouts when I step outside.

I survey the pool area. Besides two men lying on loungers, it's empty. It usually is at this time of the morning.

"Gentlemen," I greet them.

"It is Double Crown," the man repeats. He's wearing a pair of boxer shorts – not swimming trunks – and nothing else. Thankfully, the boxer shorts are a dark color.

"Course it is. He owns the place," the other man slurs. At least he's wearing a white t-shirt with his boxer shorts.

"It's time for the two of you to return to your accommodation."

"Return to our accommodation?" Boxer shorts says. "Why?"

"This pool is designated a family area during the day."

White t-shirt cracks up. "Double Crown sounds as if he has a signal pole rammed up his ass. The pool is a designated family area," he mimics.

"We're family," claims boxer shorts. "He's my brother."

They don't resemble each other in the least, but I don't contradict them. You can't argue with drunk.

"Shall I escort you to your room?"

I don't wait for an answer before helping boxer shorts to his feet. He sways and I steady him with my hand. Once I'm certain he won't collapse, I assist white t-shirt to stand.

"Thanks, Double C—" He doesn't manage to finish before he bends over and vomits all over my shoes.

Boxer shorts bursts into laughter. "You puked all over Double Crown."

"At least I didn't pee my pants." White t-shirt points to boxer shorts who is now sporting a wet spot on his shorts.

Why did I want to own a resort, again? I blame my business manager. He's the one who suggested it. He pointed out how Smuggler's Hideaway is a popular tourist destination but didn't have enough hotel rooms to accommodate tourists.

Wesley hustles to my side with two security guards. "We've got this."

I allow them to take over. I try to keep the security of the resort hidden from the guests. But this is one situation when I don't mind them handling things.

At least the incident kept Nova away from the forefront of my mind for a while. But she's never far from my thoughts.

Which is a problem I need to handle.

But first I need to throw away these shoes.

Chapter 8

Bikini – an excuse for Hudson to lose his mind

NOVA

"This is going to be fun," Chloe says as Sophia parks at the lagoon.

"I don't know about this. We have to wear mermaid tails?" Maya shivers. "I don't want anyone to see me in one."

We're at the first annual *Mermaid Lagoon Race*. I don't know who keeps coming up with fun stuff for tourists to do, but they're a genius. Last month there was a *Bootlegger Escape Room*. It was a ball. Or, rather, what I remember of it was. It involved way too many shots of moonshine.

I'm certain the *Mermaid Lagoon Race* will be as much fun if not more. Especially since there's no drinking involved. Moonshine hangovers are the worst.

I wrap an arm around Maya's shoulders. "You'll look sexy."

Chloe waggles her eyebrows. "We'll all look sexy."

Paisley studies Chloe. "You're different since you've fallen in love with your husband."

I knew Lucas couldn't resist Chloe. Not only is she beautiful but she's fiercely loyal. When she went all mama beer to protect Lucas's daughter, Natalia, Lucas fell hard and fast.

Maya sighs. "She has her happy ending."

"Yep." Chloe grins. "And I'm not even going to make fun of Maya for being a hopeless romantic."

"She's really in love," Maya whispers.

"And married." Sophia points to Chloe's wedding ring.

Chloe throws her arm around Sophia. "Don't you worry. Flynn will propose."

We exit the car and make our way to the check in for the *Mermaid Lagoon Race*.

"Hey, Sloane," I greet. Sloane is a bartender at the *Bootlegger* bar. She also does a lot of odd jobs around Smuggler's Hideaway.

"Oh boy. The troublemakers are here," she mutters.

I beam at her. "We're not always troublemakers."

"Are you forgetting about the time you broke into the manager's office at the bar? I found you there in the morning fast asleep."

I wrinkle my nose. "It was a dare."

She chuckles. "At least you were dressed unlike this one." She motions to Chloe who shrugs.

"Nothing wrong with nudity."

"Disagree," Maya mutters.

Chloe elbows her. "Don't be shy. You have a banging body. I'd kill for all those curves."

"No body shaming," I order and Chloe holds up her hands before backing away muttering sorry.

Sloane hands us each a number. "Pin these to your swimming suits." She points to a table. "You can get your mermaid tails there. The first event is the synchronized swimming competition."

"Synchronized swimming as in music plays and we do tricks the way they do in the Olympics?" Sophia asks.

Sloane groans. "I don't want to think of what act the lot of you would come up with. Probably some stripper song."

"I was thinking more *I'm too sexy*," Sophia says.

"Anyway." Sloane clears her throat. "The synchronized swimming competition is actually a race. Two mermaids have their hands tied together and swim across the lagoon."

"Chloe should do this event. She has some experience with being tied up." Sophia winks.

Chloe gasps. "How do you know?"

"My big brother's a cop. I can recognize handcuff chafe anywhere."

"This is why no one wanted the five of you on the cheerleading team," Sloane says.

"Hey! I'm offended. The lead cheerleader asked me to try out." I'm not lying. The only reason she asked was because my mom had died but still. She asked.

Sloane lifts an eyebrow. "And how did that work out for you?"

"I tripped. It happens."

"Except you tripped and literally caused the entire row of cheerleaders to fall down," Paisley says. "I believe one girl broke her wrist."

"Shall we get our mermaid tails?" I don't need to be reminded of how embarrassing my try-out was. Although, banning me from cheerleading for life was a bit over the top.

I herd everyone to the booth set up with all shapes and sizes of mermaid tails. Despite living in Smuggler's Hideaway – where believing in mermaids is the norm – my entire life, I've never seen this many mermaid tails gathered in one place.

"They're pretty," Maya murmurs as she trails her finger along the display.

"Come on," Sophia orders. "Pick out a mermaid tail and get changed. We don't want to miss the first event."

Paisley pushes her glasses up her nose. "Chloe and Nova should participate in the race. Nova's the best swimmer and Chloe's the best athlete."

I don't argue since Paisley's right.

Chloe picks out a blue tail with fish scales on it while I choose a rainbow one. We sit on a bench to put our tails on. Chloe's quicker than me. She's tall and slim. The perfect body for a mermaid.

"I think I found my Halloween costume," Chloe says as she hops to her feet.

"How are you going to trick or treat with a tail on?" I ask.

"I can hop." She proceeds to hop all the way to the starting line of the race. Paisley wasn't kidding when she said Chloe is the most athletic of us.

Meanwhile, I can't stand. I hold out my arms. "Someone help me up."

Paisley and Maya help me to stand. Sophia's eyes widen when I'm upright. "Too bad Hudson isn't here. He couldn't resist you if he saw you in this outfit. I think I have boob-envy."

I feel my cheeks heat. Hudson did enjoy playing with my breasts the night we spent together. I shiver as I recall his mouth on me giving me pleasure. For a man who hates me, he sure knows how to give a girl an orgasm.

"Hudson is not interested in me." Truth. "And I'm not interested in him." Lie. Embarrassing but true. I want the man who can't stand me.

Maya snorts. "Sure, you aren't."

"Nova, hurry up!" Chloe hollers from where she's already standing at the starting line, twirling a rope in her hands.

I try following her but my breasts bounce and nearly escape my bikini top. I never should have let my friends talk me into wearing a bikini. I should have worn my one-piece racing swimsuit. At least it has a bit of support for my breasts.

"There's no way I can hop over there."

Paisley studies me as she circles me. "We should have brought a cart dolly."

I'm not offended. She doesn't mean anything personal with her comment. She's merely computing the easiest way to get me to the starting line in her big brain.

"I'll help." Maya circles my waist with her arm and steadies me as I begin hopping to the starting line.

"We are totally gonna win this," Chloe says when we reach her.

I giggle. "My performance thus far is less than inspiring."

"Once you're in the water you'll be fine." She attaches the rope to my right arm before attaching the other end to her left arm.

The rope is about two feet long and stretches.

"You better not drown me."

"Don't worry. My handsome husband will save us." She nods to where the police and paramedics are gathered. Lucas notices her and she waves. He shakes his head in response.

"Where's Natalia?"

"She's at the beach with her friends since the *Mermaid Lagoon Races* are strictly adult."

"Contestants enter the water!" Sloane yells over a megaphone.

We grasp hands and make our way into the water. Chloe is more graceful than me. But then again, she always appears more graceful. I blame her long, lean body.

"On your mark, get set, swim like a mermaid."

I dive into the water with Chloe beside me. I swim as fast as I can while tied to another human being and wearing a mermaid tail. Although, the tail helps. Huh. Maybe I should buy one of these.

"Go Chloe! Go Nova!"

I glance to the right at the cheering and notice Sophia has pompoms she's using to cheer us on. Why am I not surprised she has pompoms? Maya and Paisley don't have any but they're cheering as well.

"Almost there," Chloe says and I return my attention to the swim.

The finish line is close. I push my legs a bit harder and Chloe falls behind. The rope pulls tight but I keep going. I can drag her if I need to. She doesn't weigh anything.

We cross the finish line and cheers erupt. We did it. We won.

Sophia, Maya, and Paisley rush into the water toward us.

"You did it!" Sophia shouts.

I lay on my back as I struggle to catch my breath while Paisley unties us.

Someone grabs me under my arms and hauls me out of the water. "What's going on?"

Hudson carries me to a bench and sets me down. "I wasn't going to watch you drown."

"I wasn't drowning. I was catching my breath. In case you missed it, I'm an awesome swimmer."

His gaze rakes my body and he scowls. It's obvious he regrets having sex with me while the night we spent together was the best sex in my life.

I need to stop obsessing about the sexy former football player. I need to let him go.

"What are you wearing?"

My brow wrinkles. "A mermaid tail. You can hardly participate in a mermaid race without a mermaid tale."

"You couldn't have worn a one-piece," he grumbles before whipping his t-shirt off. I did not exaggerate how muscular his chest is. I fist my hands before I reach out to touch him. To caress his skin. To feel how warm it is. To watch as his muscles ripple in response to my touch.

"Arms up."

At his order, I force my gaze away from his chest. "Why?"

"Arms up."

I'm ashamed to say it but my body doesn't hesitate to follow his orders. I'd probably jump off the cliff at *Mermaid Mystical Gardens* if he asked me to.

He puts his t-shirt on me. "Much better."

His t-shirt goes nearly to my knees. "I can't swim in this. I'll drown."

He grunts. "Good."

I rear back. "You want me to drown?"

"I want you to stay out of the lagoon."

"You really don't understand the concept of *Mermaid Lagoon Races.*"

"Nova!" Chloe yells. "It's time to receive our prize."

I stand and wobble since I forgot all about having on a mermaid tail. Hudson steadies me. "Be careful."

I push him away. "Stop ordering me around. You hate me. Got it. Message received."

I hop away before he has a chance to respond. I'm done listening to him tell me I'm not good enough for him.

Chapter 9

Enough – not applicable when it comes to pregnancy tests

Nova

My alarm goes off and I groan. Usually, I don't need my alarm to wake me. I'm a morning person and proud of it.

But my limbs feel tired and heavy. I want to snuggle into my covers and go back to sleep until I don't feel tired anymore.

If I'm being honest, I've been feeling tired a lot lately. The days are getting shorter and the weather is cooling down, but I don't usually have problems with the seasonal changes.

I normally love how cozy the autumn can be. Wearing thick sweaters and leggings while drinking pumpkin spice coffee and eating some pumpkin treats from *Pirates Pastries* is joyful. I do love my pumpkin.

This season is different. I'm tired all the time. Last night I went to bed before nine. And I'm still tired. It's crazy.

I roll to my side to get out of bed and my stomach protests. It gurgles and bile forms in my mouth. Oh no.

I rush to the bathroom and manage to flip the toilet lid open in time to throw up. When my stomach is finally empty, I collapse on the floor of the bathroom.

What in the world did I eat to cause this?

I wait to make certain my stomach is not on the verge of losing its contents again before standing and rummaging in my medicine cabinet. I know I have some stuff to calm an iffy stomach in here somewhere.

I push my tampons out of the way and freeze. I haven't needed these in a long while. When was the last time I had my period?

I'm not one of those women who keeps track of her period on an app, so I have no way of checking. Have I had my period since I had sex with Hudson? Am I pregnant?

My emotions war against each other.

Ecstasy fights for top billing. A baby. A family. Everything I've ever wanted since Mom died.

Fear is not to be outdone. I can't have a baby with a man who hates me. But I could go it alone. Mom did fine raising me after Dad died.

I push those thoughts away. I would never keep a baby secret from Hudson.

Hold on. There might not even be a baby.

I need to find out for sure before I have a complete meltdown. But I can't go to the pharmacy and buy a test. In a town the size of Smuggler's Rest on an equally small island, everyone will know I've bought a pregnancy test before I can make it home to actually take the test.

I need to go to the mainland where no one knows me.

I dig out my phone and dial Maya.

"Hey, Nova. Running late today?"

"Yeah," I croak out. "I don't think I'll make it in today at all."

"You're sick? Do you want me to get you some crackers and ginger ale? I can be at your house in thirty minutes."

"No!" I clear my throat and try again. "I mean no, thank you. I have everything I need in the house."

Except pregnancy tests because I wasn't exactly planning on getting pregnant with my one-night stand. I shake my head. I don't know if I am pregnant.

My periods have always been erratic and having an IUD placed didn't help regulate them. I'm probably stressing about nothing. It wouldn't be the first time.

"Okay. Let me know if you need anything."

Maya rings off and I blow out a breath in relief. She didn't question me. Maya never would. It's why I contacted my shy friend instead of anyone else.

Sophia and Chloe would badger me with questions. As would Paisley. Her questions would be out of concern, though, whereas Sophia and Chloe are just plain nosy.

I hurry to get dressed and ready to go outside. Time to figure out if I'm panicking for nothing.

It's thirty minutes to the nearest town on the mainland but I continue to the next one. It would be just my luck to bump into a fellow smuggler at a pharmacy off the island. I don't want to chance it.

I arrive in the next town after an additional fifteen minutes. I cruise slowly down the main drag until I notice a pharmacy.

I park in front of it and slip on my sunglasses before stepping out of the car. I scan the street for any familiar faces. When I don't notice any, I rush into the store. The bell rings over the door and the cashier glances over at me.

She raises her eyebrow at me and I realize I'm standing with my body plastered to the door while wearing sunglasses inside. So much for not drawing people's attention.

I grin at her before removing my sunglasses and stuffing them in my purse. I grab a basket and begin throwing random stuff in it. Shampoo, toothpaste, tortilla chips. I stop when I come to the aisle with pregnancy tests.

I read a few labels. *Test early and often. Over 99% accurate. 6 days sooner. 3 ways to test. Early result.*

I have no idea which one is the best to use. I grab one of each.

My basket is overflowing when I set it on the checkout counter. The cashier begins emptying it.

"You do know you can buy the pregnancy tests without buying any other items?"

My cheeks warm. I don't know what I was thinking. I can't disguise the tests from her. She literally has to scan them. Maybe I should have gone to a big store with self-checkout.

"I need the other items," I claim.

She holds up a box of tampons. "Really?"

I shrug. "Maybe I'm not pregnant."

She chuckles. "In my experience, when a woman of your age comes in here and buys twenty pregnancy tests, she's pregnant."

Of my age? I'm thirty not sixty.

"I didn't buy twenty."

"Shall I count?"

My cheeks are now on fire. "No."

She begins ringing up my purchases. "You have two of this brand." She sets one to the side. "And three of these."

"The packaging was confusing."

She pats my hand. "I understand."

She finishes ringing up my purchases. I pay and she hands me two large bags.

"You can take the tests in our restroom." She points to the back of the store.

"I don't know how much time I'll need."

"Don't worry about it."

I thank her before scurrying to the restroom. I lock the door behind me and empty my bags out on the counter. I separate out the pregnancy tests and shove everything else back into the bags.

Ten minutes later, I've peed on countless sticks and washed my hands several times. I should have bought some hand lotion.

Ten pregnancy tests are lined up on the counter. My alarm goes off.

I don't want to look but I have to. I have to know. Is this another one of my hypochondria attacks? Am I going overboard again? Or am I...

I read off the tests.

Pregnant.

Pregnant.

Pregnant.

Pregnant.

Pregnant.

Pregnant.

Pregnant.

Pregnant.

Pregnant.

Pregnant.

I squeal. I can't help it. I've wanted a baby ever since I can remember. Long before Mom got sick. Maybe even before Dad died.

I'll deal with the other issues – being a single mom, telling Hudson he's going to be a father – later. There's nothing I can't handle.

I let excitement rule.

No one's raining on my parade today.

Not even the baby's father.

Chapter 10

Two-minute warning – a warning Hudson's avoidance of Nova is about to come to an end

HUDSON

My feet pound the pavement as I run toward the resort. My ankle and Achilles' tendon ache but I don't stop. I may not be able to play professional football anymore, but I refuse to stop running, or lifting weights, or playing sports.

I am an athlete. It's what I do. It's who I am.

The doctors didn't think I'd be able to run again after the defensive lineman broke my ankle and ruptured my tendon. I showed them. But the months of grueling physical training were for nothing. When I returned to the team, the team doc wouldn't sign off on my return. My career was done.

I rub a hand over my chest as the familiar pain of failure hits me. The feeling keeps me awake at night.

Except for the night I spent with Nova. I didn't have any problems sleeping after burying myself deep in her body and exploding with pleasure.

My cock twitches. It doesn't understand why I refuse to give into the temptation of Nova again.

I ignore it and increase my speed until the sweat is rolling down my back and my muscles burn from the exertion. Maybe if I exhaust myself, I won't be tempted to take my cock in my hand as I shower and imagine Nova's lips around me. Nova on her knees before me. Nova with those exotic eyes staring up at me.

I sprint around the last bend to the resort and catch a glimpse of a police vehicle driving into the parking lot. Shit. What now? I hope it isn't drunk guests again. I prefer to limit having my shoes thrown up on to once in a lifetime.

I manage to catch up to the vehicle as Lucas is getting out of the driver's side.

"Lucas," I call as I come to a halt next to the car.

I bend over and rest my hands on my knees as I catch my breath. My lungs burn from how hard I pushed myself the last quarter of a mile. I don't mind. I enjoy the burn. It reminds me of what my body is capable of. Of the lengths I can push it to. Of how satisfying being an athlete can be.

"You're up early for a run."

I grunt. I'm always up early since sleeping is a luxury of my pre-injury past.

"Are you here to arrest someone?"

"He can arrest me," a woman hollers as she steps out of the main resort building.

Lucas throws up his left hand. "Married."

My brow wrinkles. His marriage is fake. He married Chloe to keep custody of his daughter. They're playing happy family until his ex-wife loses her bid for custody.

"I'll be your side piece. I don't mind." The woman isn't giving up.

Lucas doesn't bother looking at her. "Not interested."

"What about your friend?"

I nearly chuckle. I haven't been referred to as 'the friend' since the first time I stepped out on the football field.

"Not interested."

She rakes her gaze over my body. "I can give you a rub down. I'm very good with my hands."

Lucas raises an eyebrow. "I can come back later."

I grunt. I don't fuck the guests. I've hardly fucked anyone since I returned home. Except Nova. All roads lead back to her.

"Why are you here anyway?"

He grins and rocks back on his heels. "I want to book the venue."

I'm confused. His wedding was here a few months ago. In my experience, people don't book the same venue twice in the same year.

"Again? Is someone else getting married?"

He nods toward the woman who's inching closer to us as we speak. "Can we speak in private?"

"My office." I march to the entrance and the woman steps in my way. "Not interested," I grumble as I step around her.

"I'm up for a threesome. I'm a very hard worker."

"I'm married *and* I'm on duty." Lucas places his hand over his service weapon and the woman's eyes widen before she scurries away.

I escort Lucas into the building and down the hallway to my office. I motion for him to have a seat before I grab a towel and wipe the sweat from my forehead.

"Sorry," I say as I join him. "I don't usually do meetings in my sports attire."

"No worries. I wanted to catch you before most of the island wakes up since I'm trying to keep this a surprise."

"A surprise? What's going on?"

His answering smile is nearly as wide as Nova's. "I want to surprise Chloe and re-do our wedding."

I scratch my neck. "But your marriage is fake."

"Our marriage isn't fake," he insists. "I made certain Weston's mother could legally perform the marriage before the ceremony."

"Yes, of course. It's not fake but you and Chloe aren't together."

He smirks. "We are. I admit we did things out of order. I married her before I fell in love with her, but we're together now and I'm not letting her go."

My stomach burns with envy. He has the woman he wants in his bed every night whereas I only got one night with Nova. One night instead of every night.

"Congratulations," I force myself to say.

"Thanks."

"You want to re-do your wedding? Ceremony and all?"

"Not the ceremony. Just the reception."

"What date are you thinking?" I ask as I grab my tablet and open the booking software.

"As soon as the venue is available. And the honeymoon chalet is available. Our first stay in the honeymoon chalet needs a re-do, too."

Visions of Nova and how we spent the night in one of the honeymoon chalets invade my mind but I clear my throat and force them away. Getting a hard-on in front of a client is not the way I want to operate my business. Especially since these running shorts hide nothing.

"What about decorations, flowers, food?"

"I want the dinner to be exactly the same as our reception dinner."

"That simplifies things quite a bit." We settle on a date a week from now and I send the information to the event coordinator, Terri.

"If there are any issues, I'll have Terri contact you," I say as I stand.

I lead him down the hallway back to the reception area. We're nearly to the exit when the woman from earlier rushes toward us towing another woman behind her.

"I told you this place is hottie heaven."

Lucas grunts before walking out the door leaving me with the two women.

Women I'm not interested in because neither one of them is Nova.

Nova. I'm looking forward to seeing her again next week at Lucas and Chloe's reception. I bet she'll be surprised to see me again. My little ray of sunshine was not happy when I showed up at the *Mermaid Lagoon Races.*

"Boss!" Roger rushes to me from the reception desk. "I need your help."

"What is it?" I ask once we're away from the women.

"Nothing. Thought you needed an assist." He winks.

I grunt my thanks. "I need a shower."

Where I will not spend my time wondering what dress Nova will wear at the party. I will not think about Nova at all. I certainly won't imagine her in her bikini top with her breasts practically falling out for every man to see. Or her in my t-shirt after I dressed her in it.

Possessive feelings course through my veins at the memory of Nova in my t-shirt.

Nova isn't mine, I remind myself. Her sunshine is not intended for my grumpy ass.

Chapter 11

Surprise – An unexpected event. Hint. It's not the party.

NOVA

"I don't know why this party has to be at *Hideaway Haven Resort*," I complain as I drive Maya and Paisley toward the resort where Lucas has set up a surprise party for Chloe.

I don't want to return to the scene of the crime. And I definitely don't want to accidentally bump into Hudson. I glance at my belly. The conversation will have to happen but not yet.

"I think it's romantic." Maya sighs. "They're having a do-over of their wedding reception, but this time they're in love."

"I'm just glad the resort is now carrying our beer," Paisley says. "Good job on landing the account, Nova."

My cheeks heat as I remember how I landed the account. After my night spent with Hudson, I thought I'd lost the *Hideaway Haven Resort* account for good. But a man named Wesley phoned the next day from the resort to negotiate the contract.

I had no idea what he was talking about. I asked him what contract. When he finished laughing, we had a deal to provide the resort with every beer we now produce as well as any future beer we develop. I should probably thank Hudson for giving *Five Fathoms* a chance. But I won't.

"Does this mean you get to see more of the sexy owner of the resort?" Maya asks.

I scowl. "I don't want to see Hudson any more than I already do."

I can't believe he showed up at the *Mermaid Lagoon Races* to complain about me wearing a bikini. He hates me. I get it. He can stop being a jerk now.

"But you hardly ever see him."

"Which is exactly the way I want to keep it."

"I don't understand," Paisley says. "You clearly find the man attractive. Why don't you want to see him?"

Thank the smugglers in heaven, we've arrived at the resort because I am not answering her question. I park, switch off the engine, and jump out of the car. My stomach cramps and I place a hand over it. This is not the time to throw up. You'd think I threw up enough today already. You'd be wrong.

"What's your hurry?" Maya asks as she rounds the car to where I'm standing.

"We're supposed to be waiting in the lobby when Chloe and Lucas arrive."

Paisley checks the time. "They should be here any minute. Let's get inside."

The foyer is crowded with guests. I spot Sophia with Flynn and her brother Weston and join them.

"I can't believe Chloe is the second one of us to fall in love and the first one to get married. My money was on Maya," Sophia says.

Maya's cheeks heat. "I'm not in a hurry to find love," she whispers.

Weston smirks. "Because you're waiting for a certain someone to come home."

Maya ducks her chin and shrinks into herself. Her shyness goes into overdrive whenever anyone mentions Caleb.

Caleb is from Smuggler's Hideaway but he left after our high school graduation to join the Army. Maya's been pen pals with him for years. She's also had a crush on him since he helped her climb the monkey bars in second grade.

I elbow Weston. "Don't embarrass her."

He doesn't get a chance to respond before Lucas and Chloe arrive, and everyone cheers.

"Awesome. The couple is here. I've greeted them. Time to go secure some company for the evening." Weston wiggles his eyebrows before wandering off.

Sophia purses her lips. "I can't believe my brother is such a manwhore."

Flynn kisses her cheek. "I'll keep an eye on him."

"Don't forget you promised to drive home," she shouts after him.

"I can drive you home if you drink too much," I offer.

She narrows her eyes at me. "Aren't you drinking?" I shake my head. "Why not?"

I can't tell her the real reason. I'm barely eight weeks pregnant. It's too early to share my news. Too many things can go wrong in the first trimester. Considering my luck, I'm keeping the news to myself.

"Not feeling well."

She frowns but doesn't comment. My friends are the best. They never remark on my hypochondria or tell me I'm exaggerating or being dramatic.

Sophia threads her arm through my elbow. "Come on. We'll get you some seltzer water."

She leads me to the ballroom with Paisley and Maya following us.

"This is beyond romantic," Maya says when we enter.

I sigh as I look around. The place is drenched in romance. There are pale pink roses on each table. Pink balloons hang from the chandeliers. And there are more candles here than I've ever seen in one place before. Hudson's a cranky pants but his resort is the best.

"Agree. I'm happy Chloe found happiness."

Paisley nods. "Me too. She was very lonely."

"She wasn't lonely," I insist. "She had us. What else could she need?"

Maya points to Chloe and Lucas standing with his parents. "Him. She needed him."

Sophia sighs. "Since Chloe's found love, there's no one around to make fun of Maya's romantic tendencies."

Good. I'm glad. No one should make fun of Maya. She pretends it doesn't bother her, but I know it does. How could it not after how her parents acted?

Paisley studies the seating chart. "Our table is over there."

"Meet ya there. I'll get the drinks." Sophia skips off to the bar where Flynn happens to be.

"She's going to be a while," I mutter as I weave my way through the tables to ours. I read the nametags until I find my spot. I scowl when I notice who's seated next to me. "Why is Hudson invited?"

"He's a client," Paisley says.

"It's a huge account." As the financial wizard of *Five Fathoms Brewing*, Maya is well aware of how big an account the resort is.

Which is why I kept bothering Hudson to try our beers. Not to mention how much it bugged me that the biggest hotel on the island didn't want to carry beer from the local brewery. It was an insult. An insult I had no plans to accept.

My stomach flutters and I place a hand over it. Maybe I should have accepted the insult and walked away after all.

No. I will never regret baby Sprog. A sliver of panic weaves its way through my veins but I shove it away. I refuse to panic about Sprog's chance of survival during Chloe's surprise party.

"Here, we go." Sophia arrives with a bottle of champagne and four glasses.

I hold up my hand when she tries to hand a glass to me. "I'm driving."

"And she hasn't been feeling well," Maya adds.

I smile to hide my annoyance. She's not supposed to tell anyone I haven't been feeling well. Although I didn't make her promise to keep quiet. Maybe I should have.

Sophia hands me a glass of ginger ale. "Here you go, spoilsport."

"I'm not a spoilsport."

"No, she's not." Paisley points to my stomach. "She's pregnant."

I gasp. "How do you know?"

Sophia slams her glass on the table. "It's true? Why does Paisley know and I don't?"

Maya holds up her hand. "I didn't know either. I mean, I suspected. But I didn't actually know."

Sophia narrows her eyes on Maya. "You suspected?"

Maya motions to me. "She's been throwing up every morning at work. Haven't you noticed?"

And here I thought I was keeping my morning vomiting sessions a secret. I guess not.

"I have," Paisley says. "I also noticed she hasn't been drinking. Not even champagne to celebrate our friend's marriage, which could only mean one thing."

I might as well admit it. "I'm pregnant."

"Yes." She nods. "The question I want to know the answer to is who is the father of your baby."

"You're pregnant! Who the fuck is the father?" Hudson shouts, and I cringe. Where did he come from? "Were you fucking him when we were together?"

I stand to face him. "Can you please stop shouting the f-word?"

He gets in my face. "Who is the father of your baby?"

I push him away. "Do not shout in my face."

"Fuck. Sorry."

I glare at him. "Do you know any words besides the f-word?"

"Do you know who the father of your baby is?"

He can't be serious. Does he think I'm a slut? Before I know what's happening, my hand is slapping his face.

"You are, you jerk. I don't sleep around."

He captures my hand. "Let's go."

"Go? I'm not going anywhere with you."

He leans down to whisper in my ear. "Do you want to discuss how you're carrying my baby in front of the entire island?"

I scan the room. Sure enough. Everyone in the place is watching and listening. Even Chloe is making her way across the room with a smirk on her face.

"Fine. We'll discuss this in private. But I don't need you to drag me." I wrench my hand from his hold.

"Follow me." He leads the way to a door marked *private*.

I wasn't planning on revealing my pregnancy to my friends let alone discussing the situation with the father of the baby today but I no longer have a choice. I eye the patio door leading to the deck and pool area. Unless I decide to make a run for it.

Nope. I'm not a runner.

I straighten my back. I can do this. I've survived much worse.

Chapter 12

Audible – When Hudson changes the rules before Nova has a chance to protest

HUDSON

I usher Nova into the event coordinator's office. Luckily, Terri isn't in here. Nova scurries past me to the other side of the room and I lock the door.

I cross my arms over my chest and glare at her. "You're pregnant?"

She places a protective hand over her stomach. "Yes."

I grit my teeth. She's pregnant and didn't tell me.

"Were you even going to tell me? Or were you going to have this baby without me? My kid would be growing up on this island where I live and I wouldn't know it."

She holds up a hand. "Slow down. I was planning to tell you."

"Oh yeah? When? When were you planning to tell me? It's been eight weeks."

I remember exactly how long it's been. How can I not? I think about my night with Nova every night in my bed.

Usually with my cock in my hand because Nova is not only sweet and full of sunshine. She's also sexy as hell. Being with her was the best sex of my life.

"Exactly. It's been eight weeks."

I blink. "What?"

She blows out a breath. "The chance of miscarriage is highest in the first trimester. I wasn't planning on telling anyone until the first trimester was over."

There's one flaw in her argument. "Your friends know."

"They guessed. Pro tip. Never try to keep a secret from Paisley. The genius woman will figure it out."

"But you were planning to tell me?" I know I'm harping on this point but it's important. The idea of *my* kid being out there in the world and not knowing about me burns.

"I would never keep a child a secret from his father even if the father hates me."

I frown. "I don't hate you."

"Really?" She snorts. "You sure act as if you do. Nova, don't wear that dress. It's unattractive. Nova, don't wear a bikini. Nova, your brewery isn't good enough for my resort. Not to mention all the times you've hung up on me."

I don't hate Nova. I could never hate her. She's sunshine and happiness and everything I'm not.

"I don't hate you."

"Why? Because I'm your baby mamma?"

"Yes."

She shakes her head. "I don't want you to act as though you like me for the benefit of baby Sprog."

"Sprog?"

She shrugs. "I can't call the baby it."

I should have known she'd come up with a cute name for the baby. Everything about Nova is cute. Even her panties are cute. I wonder what panties she's wearing now. My cock twitches. It wants to know. It wants to know everything about Nova.

"Anyway." She clears her throat. "I don't expect anything from you. You don't have to be involved in any way. I don't need your money either."

"My money?" I growl.

She waves a hand in the air. "You know what I mean. Child support or whatever it's called. I don't need it. I'm comfortable."

She's starting to piss me off.

"I will be involved with this child's life. And if I want to give you money to support our child, I will."

Her nostrils flare. Damn. Nova pissed off is sexy. My cock agrees. I clench my jaw. This is not the time to get excited.

"I don't need your money."

"I never said you did."

"Maybe not but you've made it perfectly obvious you think I'm not good enough for you."

Her, not good enough for me? She's got it all wrong. I'm the one who isn't good enough for her.

"I never said you aren't good enough."

"Actions speak louder than words."

I prowl toward her. "And what did my actions say the night Sprog was conceived?"

She places a hand on her stomach and I skid to a halt. She's pregnant. I need to be gentle with her. I need to take care of her. Speaking of which.

"We should get married."

Her eyes widen. "What?"

"We should get married. Sprog can grow up with his parents in the same house."

"I'm not marrying you because I'm pregnant. I'm not some football groupie who tricked you into getting pregnant to force you to marry me."

Which leads to my next question. "How did you get pregnant?"

Her nose wrinkles. "Um, the usual way. We had sex."

"I know we had sex."

How could I forget? I can't. I can't forget how she tastes. How she feels. How she looks when she comes. It's tattooed on my brain. "You said you were on birth control."

"I am." She doesn't hesitate. "I have an IUD. I plan to ask the doctor what happened."

I cross my arms over my chest and her gaze drops to them. Her eyes flare and I can't help myself. I flex my biceps. She bites her bottom lip. What I wouldn't give to be the man who has the right to pull her lip from her teeth and plunder her mouth.

But I'm not that man. I don't want to blemish her sunshine. I want her to shine bright.

"My offer still stands. We can get married."

"I'm not Chloe. I'm not having a fake marriage. When I get married, it'll be real. We'll be in love and unable to keep our hands off each other."

I can barely keep my hands to myself now. But Nova doesn't know how tempting she is.

"Okay. We won't get married."

"Good. The matter's settled then." She tries to scoot around me, but I shackle her wrist to stop her.

"You're still pregnant."

She beams up at me. "Yes, I am."

"You're happy about this."

"I want a family. I'm sad Sprog won't have a grandma or grandpa, but I'll make it up to him. My mom raised me alone and I turned out pretty darn good."

Better than good. But she's wrong.

"Sprog will have a grandma and grandpa. And lots of uncles."

Her brow wrinkles. "What?"

"My parents will be great grandparents. My brothers will probably be dangerous uncles. If Sprog is a girl, we probably shouldn't let them babysit."

Her mouth drops open. "Your parents? Your brothers?"

I close her mouth with my finger. Her smooth skin tempts me but I manage to drop my hand. I stick my hands in my pockets to make sure they don't stray back to Nova without my permission.

"I'm not keeping my child a secret from my family."

"Of course not." She clears her throat. "I wasn't thinking. I've been alone for such a long time, I guess, I forgot."

I fucking hate how she didn't even consider my family because she's used to being alone. Nova shouldn't be alone. She should be surrounded by beauty and love. All the things I can't give her.

"I'm sorry about your parents." The words are inadequate, but I don't know what else to say. What do you say to a woman who lost her family before she graduated high school?

Pain flashes in her eyes and she ducks her chin. "Thank you."

She blows out a breath and her smile is back. It doesn't reach her eyes this time. "Your parents won't be upset with me for getting pregnant?"

"My parents are pretty laid back. It's a requirement when you have five boys in the house causing chaos."

"Five boys? I bet your house was full of laughter and love."

I shrug. "My brothers are a decade younger than me. Mom got pregnant with me in high school. She and Dad stayed together but they decided not to have any more children until they were older."

"Your mom got pregnant with you in high school?" I nod. "Phew. She won't be mad at me for getting pregnant by accident then."

"I already told you she wouldn't."

"Great. But I'd appreciate it if you don't tell her until I'm in my second trimester."

I cough to hide my amusement. "You yelled at me in front of everyone at this reception dinner. The whole town knows by now."

She scowls. "I didn't yell at you."

"And you slapped me."

Her cheeks darken. "I'm sorry. I shouldn't have slapped you. I promise I won't use violence again." She shakes out her hand. "I've never slapped a person before. I didn't realize how much it hurts."

"Apology accepted." I capture her hand and study it. "It's a bit red but not swollen. You'll be fine."

"You have experience slapping people?"

"Not slapping but I've taken my fair share of punches and kicks."

Her eyes flare and I realize I'm caressing her hand. I drop it and retreat a few steps.

"We should probably return to the party before my friends combust from curiosity. I bet they nearly peed their pants when they found out you're the father."

She didn't tell her friends we had sex? Does she want to keep me a secret? Am I her dirty little secret?

She points to my forehead. "Whatever you're thinking stop. Sprog will come out growling at this rate."

I motion to the door. I'd rather stay in here surrounded by her wildflower scent but my control is on a razor thin edge now. Knowing my baby is growing in Nova's stomach is intoxicating.

My cock hardens and lengthens. It knows what it wants.

Too bad. Nova is not for me. Baby or not.

Chapter 13

Pushy and sweet – a combination Nova finds difficult to resist

NOVA

I groan and curl into a ball on my bed. I thought morning sickness would improve as my pregnancy progressed but it hasn't yet. Fingers crossed the second trimester will be better.

I message Maya.

> **I'm sick. I'll be in later.**

> **Maya: You better be. I have questions.**

> **Sophia: Correction. We have questions.**

So much for keeping the conversation between Maya and me.

> **Chloe: Lots and lots of questions.**

I'm certain they do. I'm also certain I don't plan to answer their questions.

When Hudson and I finished our little talk Saturday at Chloe's party, I snuck out and drove home. By the miracles of mermaids, my girlfriends let me be yesterday. I expected them to storm into my house and demand answers.

> **Me: Later.**

> **Paisley: I have some ideas to help with your nausea.**

I love my nerdy friend. She won't push me.

> **Me: Thanks. I'm going to take a nap. I'll come into work later.**

> **Maya: No rush.**

I throw my phone onto my nightstand and nestle into the covers. Hopefully I'll feel better after a few extra hours of sleep. I'm afraid I can never get enough sleep, though. Growing a baby is exhausting.

Bang! Bang! Bang!

I startle awake at the sound of banging on my front door. I glance at the clock. It's nearly noon. I guess my friends decided they were done waiting for answers to their questions.

I haul myself out of bed and stumble down the hallway to open the door.

"Why are you banging on the door? You have a key."

"I don't have a key but a key is a good idea," Hudson says, and I jump.

"I thought you were Maya."

He smirks. "I've never been confused with a girl before."

I scowl. "Maya is a woman. Not a girl."

He clears his throat. "Of course. My apologies. Can I come in?"

He doesn't wait for my response before barreling his way past me into my house. He sets a bag down on the kitchen counter and begins unpacking it. "I brought you some essentials. Pre-natal vitamins, ginger ale, crackers, and all the ingredients for chicken noodle soup. Mom said you might be feeling nauseous and—"

"Mom? You told your mom already?"

I wasn't ready to tell him about baby Sprog, let alone his parents. They're going to hate me for ruining Hudson's life.

He grins. "She had already heard through the smuggler's grapevine. She's excited to be a grandma. She's also surprised I'm the son who's giving her, her first grandchild. She was convinced my younger brother, Brooks, would be the first to knock up a girlfriend."

"Knock up a girlfriend?"

"Brooks is a bit of a player. I had to give him the condom talk when he was thirteen."

"The condom talk? Thirteen?"

"If Sprog is a boy, I'm prepared to do the talk. But if she's a girl?" He grimaces. "You'll be up to bat for the talk then."

My knees nearly give out. He's going to be around to give my child the sex talk? I haven't thought through Hudson's involvement in the baby's life. I was too afraid the man who hates me would abandon his child.

"Where do you want these?" He waves a box of crackers at me. "In the pantry or left out in case of emergency?"

"What is happening?" Am I having a super realistic dream? Am I still in bed sleeping?

Hudson's brow wrinkles. "What do you mean? I'm helping you."

"Helping me?"

He motions to my stomach. "With the baby."

"I thought your involvement wouldn't begin until Sprog arrives."

He grunts. "My involvement starts now."

My chest warms at the determination in his voice. Hudson wants to be involved. I worried he'd wake up yesterday morning and decide to wash his hands of me and the baby. But he didn't. He's here.

"You're not obligated to get involved until Sprog is born."

He growls as he prowls toward me. He palms my neck and squeezes. "I'm not letting you go through pregnancy alone, Sunshine."

I bristle. "Not letting me?"

"I've been researching pregnancy. It's not an easy time for a woman."

My jaw drops open. "You've been researching pregnancy?"

He ignores my question. "I don't want you to be alone through this time. I want to support you."

"I have my friends," I argue.

I can't rely on Hudson. I can't depend on him. My body may yearn for him, but he's only here because I got pregnant. He doesn't want *me*. He wants to be involved in his child's life. Not mine.

"And now you have me too." He kisses my forehead before stepping away and returning to the groceries. "Now, where do you want these?"

Huh? What? I have no idea what he's talking about. I'm too busy feeling all warm and gooey from a kiss on the forehead.

Pull yourself together, Nova. The grumpy resort owner is not the man for you. He's here because of the baby. A week ago, he would have scurried the other way if he saw me coming.

"I'll put them away later."

He glares at me. "Where do you want these?"

"Grumpy McGrumperson has returned to the island."

He shakes the crackers at me. "Where?"

I blow out a breath. "The pantry is fine."

He scans the area until his gaze lands on the small door next to my kitchen table. He places the ginger ale and boxes of crackers on a shelf.

"Now," he says when he's finished. "Have you eaten?"

I shake my head.

He frowns. "It's nearly noon and you haven't eaten yet. You need to take better care of yourself."

"Easy for you to say. You didn't spend hours throwing up this morning."

"It's normal to feel nauseous in the first trimester."

I blink. "What?"

"I told you I've been researching."

"I…" My response is cut off when my stomach rumbles. Loudly. Great. This conversation wasn't awkward enough.

"Sit," Hudson orders.

When I stare at him, he walks over to me, picks me up, and places me on a barstool.

"Stay there."

"I'm not a dog."

"No. You're the woman growing my baby. You need to rest and let someone else care for you for a change."

It's a good thing I'm sitting because those words would have me melting into a puddle on the floor. No one's taken care of me in a long time. Even when Mom was still alive, it was me taking care of her for the last months of her life while she fought cancer.

I have my friends. They're the best friends a girl could ask for. But their idea of taking care of me is grilling me over when I had sex with Hudson and why I didn't tell them.

"What do you want to eat? I can make you chicken noodle soup."

Chicken noodle soup does sound good. "The can opener is in the drawer next to the stove and there are microwave-proof bowls next to the microwave."

"I'm not feeding you soup from a can."

My nose wrinkles. "You can cook?"

"I told you I'm the oldest of five sons. Mom didn't always have time to cook considering she was raising four hellions and working full-time."

"Four hellions? Not five?"

"Between football practice, going to the gym to lift weights, running every day, and helping to raise my brothers, I didn't have time to be a hellion."

"But you did have time to date every cheerleader in high school." I nearly slap a hand over my mouth when I realize how jealous I sound. But Hudson doesn't appear to notice.

"There wasn't a whole lot of dating. There were a few girls who insisted on helping me with my homework. They referred to our library study sessions as dates."

And bragged to the entire school population about how they were dating the great Hudson Clark. I was beyond jealous of those girls. For nothing as it turns out.

He hands me a packet of crackers. "Here. Nibble on these while I cook."

He finds a cutting board and knife and begins chopping celery and carrots. I'm fascinated as he prepares the soup. It's obvious he's comfortable in the kitchen as he chops and sautés.

"Did your mom teach you how to cook?"

He pours the broth into the pan before answering. "She taught me how to chop and sauté when she had time on the weekends. During the week, she'd write me notes with very detailed instructions on how to prepare dinner."

"You can follow instructions?" I tease.

His eyes heat. "I can follow instructions when I'm interested in the results."

I squirm in my seat as I remember how I ordered him around when we had sex during the night we conceived Sprog. I shove a cracker into my mouth before I instruct him to get to his knees and deal with the ache I feel whenever he's around.

I place my hand over my stomach. I can't give in to temptation. I need to think of Sprog.

Because no matter how sweet and sexy Hudson looks in the kitchen. He's not here for me. He's here because of the baby.

Chapter 14

Scramble – When Hudson runs around, trying not to get sacked by Nova

HUDSON

I turn down the aisle in the grocery store and nearly bump into Weston.

"Hey, Huddy."

I grunt. I don't have time for small talk. I need to finish up these groceries for Nova and drop them at her house before getting back to the resort for a management meeting.

"I didn't expect to see you here."

I frown. "Doing groceries," I grumble before passing him.

"I thought you'd be at the hospital."

I halt. "At the hospital?"

He frowns. "I thought you were a better man than this."

I've had enough of his riddles. "What the fuck is going on?"

His eyes widen. "You don't know."

"I don't know what?"

"Nova's at the hospital."

I drop the grocery basket and rush toward the exit.

"No speeding," Weston shouts after me.

I ignore him as I break into a run. Is Nova okay? What about the baby? I jump into my vehicle, switch on the engine before I manage to shut the door, and peel out of the parking lot.

The hospital isn't far. It's on the road between Smuggler's Rest and Rogue's Landing. I park as close to the entrance as possible before rushing inside.

"Nova Myers. Where is she?" I ask the nurse at the reception desk.

"Hey, Hudson," she greets. "Nova called you?"

Acid churns in my stomach. Nova didn't call and apparently everyone on the island knows she's here except me. She didn't contact me. That shit stops now.

"Where is she?"

"Exam room two."

I march to the room. I know exactly where exam room two is. You can't be an athlete and not be familiar with the emergency room. I scowl as I remember the last emergency room I was in. But this is not the time to dwell on how my life was ruined.

I barge into the room. Nova is lying on the exam table. Her face is pale. She looks small and scared.

"What happened? Where's the doctor? Are you okay? Will you be staying overnight? How's the baby?"

A tear rolls down her cheek and I hurry to her side. I wipe the tear from her face.

"It's okay, Sunshine. We'll figure this out. We'll get you the best care money can buy."

"Ahem." A woman standing at the door clears her throat. "Are you questioning my medical skills, Hudson?"

"I wouldn't dare, Doctor Allens." I know the doctor from when I was in high school. She patched me up more times than I care to remember. "But Nova is getting the best care possible."

"I heard the baby was yours but I wasn't sure I believed it."

I scowl. I know I'm not good enough for Nova but I didn't expect the doctor to point it out. "The baby is mine."

"The baby is ours," Nova corrects.

"What happened? Why are you at the hospital? And why didn't you call me?"

She cringes. "I panicked."

I grasp her hand and squeeze. "About what? Are you okay now?"

She places her free hand over her stomach. "I'm okay. As long as Sprog is okay, I'm okay."

Nova is avoiding my questions about what happened. I can better ask the doctor. Doctor Allens doesn't lie. Not even to your parents when you beg her not to tell them about your latest football injury.

"Doctor Allens, can you explain what happened?"

The doctor raises an eyebrow at Nova who sighs. "You can tell him. He's the baby's father, after all."

She opens her chart. "Nova was worried she was losing the baby due to excessive bleeding."

Panic seizes me at the thought of Nova alone and bleeding, worried she lost the baby. I don't want her to be alone. She's been alone too much in her life already. Not anymore. Now she has me.

"Is the baby okay?"

The doctor grins. "The baby is fine and some bleeding is normal during pregnancy."

Nova's cheeks darken. "I know but what's some and what's too much?"

"You should speak to your OB/GYN about the specifics in your case."

"Do we have an OB/GYN?" I ask Nova.

"Yes, *I* have an OB/GYN."

She's cute. She thinks emphasizing the I will have an effect on me. It won't. She won't be going to any doctor's appointments without me. She's not alone. Not anymore.

"What now?" I ask Doctor Allens. "Does Nova need to spend the night at the hospital?"

She flips the chart closed. "She's free to go home. I'll have the nurse bring in the paperwork."

"Thanks, Doc."

She waves as she exits the room.

"How did you find out I'm here?" Nova asks before I have a chance to speak.

"I should have found out from you." I need to figure out a way to ensure I'm the first person she calls.

"Answer the question."

"Weston told me."

She buries her face in her hands. "Weston's a gossip. He'll have told the entire town by now."

I pinch her chin and tilt her face up. "There's nothing to be ashamed about. You were worried and went to the hospital."

"Except I was speeding and Weston pulled me over."

"No more speeding."

"Don't tell me what to do."

I place a hand over her stomach. "You have precious cargo on board. I don't want you getting into an accident."

She lets out a breath. "You're right. But I was nervous. I didn't want to be too late to get to the hospital."

"You should have called me. I would have picked you up and brought you here."

She rolls her eyes. "I'm not going to call you for every single little thing."

"Little thing?" I motion to the room. "Look at where you are at."

Her cheeks flame. "I overreacted again. The medical personnel are probably making fun of me."

"No one will make fun of you."

"What are you going to do? Be my bodyguard wherever I go and make sure no one speaks to me in a manner you don't approve of?"

I scratch my neck as I consider the matter. I have the perfect solution but Nova is not going to like it.

She slaps my chest. "You are not shadowing me the entire time I'm pregnant."

I shrug. "The idea has merit."

"Do you know what a boundary is?"

"The football field has boundaries."

"A personal boundary," she corrects.

If she's worried about personal boundaries now, she's going to lose her mind when I tell her what I have planned. Nova is going to kick my ass. But I don't care. Her safety, the baby's safety, is more important.

The nurse bustles in carrying a bundle of papers. "The doctor says you're free to go." She stumbles to a halt when she notices me. "I thought you said you didn't know who the baby daddy is."

I growl. It's one thing not to call me. It's an entirely different thing to pretend I don't exist.

"The baby is mine," I growl. "As you very well know."

There's no way the news of Nova carrying my baby escaped her. Smuggler's Hideaway is a bed of gossip. News spreads faster than my brother Owen can sneak out of the house on this island.

She giggles. "This is going to be fun."

Nova signs her release paperwork. "I'm ready to go."

I help her out of the bed and into a wheelchair.

"I can walk."

"But you're my queen and I'll push you." I push the wheelchair before she has a chance to protest again.

When we reach the exit, I aim the wheelchair toward my truck.

"My car is on the other side of the parking lot."

"Give me your keys and I'll have someone pick it up for you."

"My keys? I don't need to give you my keys. I can drive myself."

I stop the wheelchair next to my truck and kneel in front of her. "You are not driving home." She opens her mouth to protest and I hold up a hand. "You rushed to the hospital because you were sick and worried about the baby. I'm not letting you drive."

She crosses her arms over her chest. "Not letting me?"

"Let me re-phrase. I would be honored to chauffeur you and make sure you're safe."

She sighs. "Fine."

I don't give her a chance to change her mind. I open the door and lift her into the passenger seat. I reach over her and secure her seatbelt before shutting the door. I hurry to return the wheelchair since I wouldn't put it past Nova to sneak off on me.

But when I return to my truck, she's waiting for me. She has her arms across her chest and she's scowling, but she's waiting.

If she's annoyed I'm driving her home, she's going to be even more annoyed when she realizes where we're going. Too bad for her I won't budge on the destination.

Chapter 15

Poopy diapers – a reason for Nova to fall in love

NOVA

"You're going the wrong way," I tell Hudson when he turns left out of the parking lot of the hospital.

His response? He grunts.

"A grunt is not a response, Captain Cranky."

He sighs. "We're not going the wrong way."

"I think I know the way from my house to the hospital."

The smuggler knows I've driven it enough times. Between Dad and Mom being sick and my own irrational fears for my health, I've seen the inside of the Smuggler's Hideaway hospital more times than I care to admit.

"We're not going to your house."

It's like pulling teeth with this man. "Where are we going?"

"To my place."

A current of excitement travels through me. Hudson is practically a hermit. He doesn't invite people over. But he's bringing me to his place. Me? The woman who he couldn't stand less than a week ago.

I wonder what his place looks like. A typical bachelor pad? Or a sterile hotel room?

I squash those thoughts. I don't want to see Hudson's place. I want to go home. I ignore the tiny voice in my mind shouting I'm a liar. I'm not lying. I do want to go home.

"Why are we going to your house?" A thought occurs to me and I nearly thump my forehead with realization. There must be an emergency. Why else would he bring me to his house? I'm not special to him.

"Is there an emergency? You can drop me off at the side of the road. I'll have one of my girlfriends pick me up."

"I am not dropping you at the side of the road."

"It's fine. It's not raining."

"I am not dropping you at the side of the road. I'm taking care of you."

Hudson needs to stop taking care of me. He needs to stop bringing me groceries and preparing me soup. He needs to stop rushing to my side when I'm in the hospital. He needs to stop, period.

Because if he doesn't, I'm going to fall in love with this man. Which would be a disaster of mermaid proportions since the man couldn't stand me until he found out I was pregnant.

"You don't need to take care of me because you're the father of the baby I'm carrying."

"Okay," he grumbles.

Okay? Isn't he going to say more? Explain himself perhaps. I wait a few seconds but he doesn't elaborate.

"Can't you drop me off real quick at my house before you rush off to whatever emergency there is at the resort?"

"No emergency."

"No emergency?" My brow wrinkles. "Why are we going to the resort if there isn't an emergency?"

He grunts again.

I wag my finger at him. "A grunt is not an answer, Sir Grunts-a-Lot."

"I'll tell you when we arrive."

"Why not tell me now? Is it a secret? Are you afraid your truck is bugged?"

"My truck is bugged?"

"Aha! You are afraid your truck is bugged."

He barks out a laugh but coughs to cover it up. "My truck is not bugged. Why would my truck be bugged?"

"I don't know. Why won't you explain yourself in the truck if it's not bugged?"

"I won't explain myself and you jump to the conclusion that my truck is bugged?"

What can I say? If jumping to conclusions was an Olympic sport, I'd be a gold-medal contender. I probably shouldn't admit that to Hudson, though. The grump puts up with me because I'm carrying his child. He doesn't need to know about all of my issues.

I rub a hand over my belly. Although, I think he's got the hypochondriac issue figured out by now.

His gaze catches on my hand. "Are you okay? Do you want to return to the hospital?"

I snort. "Ah, no. I prefer to limit my hospital visits to one a day."

"If you need to go to the hospital, we're going."

He switches on his turn signal, but I reach across the console and grab his wrist to stop him.

"I promise I don't need the hospital."

He studies me for a moment before switching off the turn signal and continuing straight down the road to his resort.

"Why did you decide to establish *Hideaway Haven Resort*?"

He shrugs. "It was a good business opportunity. There weren't enough hotels on Smuggler's Hideaway to accommodate the number of tourists."

I tuck my ankle beneath my knee and swivel to face him. Hudson isn't much of a talker. I've got him talking now, though. I'm not one to waste an opportunity.

"But why an upscale resort?"

"My business manager suggested it."

"You have a business manager?"

He nods.

"Do you enjoy managing the resort?"

He shrugs.

I guess he's done talking.

"You've obviously been successful. You added several chalets to the property this year."

"The chalets were always part of the plan."

"Really? Cool. Paisley drafted the business plan for *Five Fathoms Brewing* but we don't have a second phase. Make beer. Sell it at the restaurant. End of plan."

"And distribute it all over the East Coast."

"I can't believe people in New York City and Miami are drinking our beer, but they are."

"It's good beer."

I clutch my chest. "Did Mr. Grouchypants give me a compliment? The shock!" I dissolve into giggles at my own joke.

"We're here," Hudson announces as he turns into a driveway. He continues driving until we reach a chalet in the woods. It reminds me of the other chalets at the resort. One chalet in particular comes to mind. My body warms as I'm reminded of all the dirty things Hudson did to me there.

Hudson parks the truck and I grasp the handle.

"No," he barks.

"No, what? You want me to wait in the truck? I can wait in the truck." I dig out my phone. "I need to call my girls and tell them I won't be in to work today anyway."

"You're not waiting in the truck."

"Maybe I should rename you Mr. Confusing. You tell me to wait in the truck and then complain I can't wait in the truck. Confusing."

"I didn't tell you to wait in the truck. I want to open your door for you."

"Oh."

Hudson reaches over to shut my mouth. "Gentlemen open doors for women."

I scan the area. "Where's this gentleman you speak of?"

His lips tip up in a near smile.

"You smiled! I win!"

He shakes his head before exiting the vehicle. I watch as he rounds the front to get to my door. I could watch Hudson walk all day. There's a reason the man was voted sexiest NFL player three years in a row.

He opens the door and I reach for his hand. But he doesn't accept it. He lifts me into his arms and carries me to the front door of his chalet.

"I'd protest I can walk but being carried is too nice. Lead me into your home, peasant man!"

He unlocks the door with a flip of his wrist and sets me on my feet in the foyer. I glance around the room.

"Holy mermaids swimming in the sea! This place is awesome."

I may be prone to exaggeration but not this time. The chalet is similar to the one we spent the night in but it's at least twice the size. It's an open concept and it is huge. The wraparound sofa in the living area probably seats twenty. Ten if they're Hudson-sized.

In the middle of the open area is a table for ten. Next to the table is the kitchen. The kitchen countertops stretch to the opposite end of the chalet. I hurry to the glass doors there.

"There's no pool."

If I sound disappointed, it's because I am. I seriously love pools.

"I love to swim. Someday I'm going to earn enough to have a pool installed in my back yard."

"We live on an island. You can swim in the ocean."

I rear back. "Swim in the ocean? No way. Sand gets everywhere and the salt dries out your skin. Give me a pool any day. I love the smell of chlorine in the morning."

"You're a nutcase."

I bow. "Thank you. My mission here is complete. Speaking of complete, why are you still here? Why aren't you handling whatever it is you urgently need to handle so I can get home?"

I don't know why I'm complaining. This place is more awesome than visiting a mermaid in her house in Atlantis.

"Um." Hudson scratches his neck. "I want you to stay here until Sprog is born."

I pretend to clean out my ears. "You want me to stay here until Sprog is born?"

"I can't take care of you if you're on the other side of the island."

I roll my eyes. "I'm fifteen minutes away."

"Fifteen minutes is too long if you need me."

Oh no. I'm in danger of melting into a puddle of goo on his perfectly oiled wooden floors. Mr. Crabby isn't supposed to want to take care of me.

"I have everything you need here. A cleaner comes in every other day. The refrigerator and pantry are stocked with food. You can order whatever you want from the resort's restaurant or I'll cook for you. You can use the gym and all the other facilities at the resort. There are several pools."

I nearly groan with how wonderful it all sounds. I can cook, but I don't enjoy it. And cleaning is my least favorite thing in the world, especially since the cleaning liquids now make me gag.

"You don't need to do this."

"Yes, I do."

I roll my eyes. "Just because I'm having your baby doesn't mean you need to switch into caveman mode."

He stalks toward me until he's within reaching distance. He tucks a strand of hair behind my ear. "I'm not doing this just for Sprog. I want you to be taken care of, too."

"And once Sprog is born, I'll return to my house?"

He shrugs. "If you want to, but you have to admit it'd be handy if you lived here. I could help with midnight feedings and poopy diapers."

My mouth drops open. "You're going to change poopy diapers?"

"Bring it on. It won't be my first poopy diaper. I practically raised my younger brothers. And Sawyer refused to be potty trained."

"You're serious." He wants us to live together after the baby's born. We could raise the baby together. We'd be a family. An unusual family since Mommy and Daddy wouldn't be together. But still. A family.

Uh oh. I'm not *going* to fall in love with Hudson sometime in the future. I already am.

Chapter 16

Tackle – What Hudson wishes he could do to a cat

HUDSON

I hold my breath as I wait for Nova to reply. I know moving in with me is a big deal for her. My sunshine girl has an independent streak a mile wide.

But I want her here. I don't want to worry she's all alone and not feeling well with no one to take care of her. I'll take care of her. Baby or not. She needs someone to be there for her.

"You stay here and relax. I'll go pick up your stuff."

"I didn't say I'm staying."

I grunt and she wags her finger at me. "Don't grunt at me, Mr. Cranksville."

Her admonishment isn't serious since she's smiling at me. Her smile hits me right in the chest. I want to smile in return. I shake my head. I'm not a smiler.

"You know you want to stay here. You practically drooled when I mentioned a housekeeper."

"I'll have you know I limit my drooling to chocolate and other yummy treats from *Pirates Pastries*."

I know another time when she drools. A time when we were naked and she was staring at my naked chest. My blood heats and my cock twitches as memories of our night together flash through my mind.

I clear my throat and tell my cock to calm the hell down. There will be no repeats of that night. My cock protests but I ignore it. The same way I've been ignoring the urge to go to Nova ever since our night together.

The woman is not for me. I'm a washed up has-been. She's sunshine and beauty and life and laughter. I refuse to ruin her goodness.

"I'll pick you up some pastries on my way home."

She sighs. "Fine. I'll stay here. But only until Sprog is born."

Which gives me a little over thirty weeks to convince her to stay after the baby is born.

"I'll be back." I make my way toward the door.

"Don't forget Finn Fable," she hollers after me.

I glance over my shoulder at her. "Finn Fable?"

She grins. "My cat."

"You have a cat?"

She blinks her eyes and feigns innocence. "What? Don't you like cats?"

I hate cats. But I'll put up with one for her. I'm discovering I'll put up with a lot for her.

"I'll get the cat."

"He's a bit shy of strangers. He may hide on you."

Great. The cat I don't want is going to hide from me.

"I'll get the cat," I repeat because I can't deny Nova anything she wants. She wants her cat. She's getting her cat. "I'll be back."

"I'll be back," she says in a robotic voice.

I hurry away before she notices my humor. The last thing I need is for Nova to know how much of an effect she has on me. Not when I can't keep her.

When I arrive at Nova's house, I notice a car that isn't hers in the driveway. I scowl. People shouldn't be using her driveway. Knowing my sunshine, she lets people use her driveway. She's always helping people out.

I park behind the car and make my way to the door. It opens before I can reach it.

"He's here!" Sophia shouts and the rest of Nova's girlfriends – Chloe, Maya, and Paisley – rush to the door.

"Why are you here?"

"Nova messaged. She was worried you forgot a key to her place," Sophia says.

Shit. I can hardly admit I swiped the extra key from Nova's kitchen drawer now.

"She also asked us to pack up her bras and panties," Chloe adds. "She wants them to be a surprise for you."

"Okay."

"Aha!" Sophia shouts. "He didn't deny he'll be seeing her bras and panties. I knew it. He wants Nova."

"Of course, he wants Nova. She's pregnant with his child," Paisley says.

Maya gives me a thumbs-up from where she's hiding behind Paisley. I lift my chin at her and she ducks behind her friend.

"Nova is not the woman for me," I say before pushing my way past them inside the house.

"Why not?" Sophia asks.

I ignore her question. "Do you have her things packed up?"

Maya points to a lone suitcase on the living room floor.

My brow wrinkles. "Is this all? This is not enough clothes for nearly seven months." I march toward her bedroom. "Does she have more suitcases? I'll just pack up all her clothes."

"All of her clothes?" Sophia screeches as she rushes to follow me.

When I enter Nova's bedroom, there are already several suitcases open on her bed. I scowl. Are Nova's girlfriends fucking with me?

Chloe herds me out of the room. "We'll finish packing. You find Finn Fable and get him settled in his cat carrier."

"Can't you get the cat?"

Chloe frowns. "Finn doesn't like me."

"Maybe because you attempted to drown him," Paisley says.

"I didn't try to drown him. How was I supposed to know he was going to jump into the toilet?"

"You didn't need to flush."

Chloe shrugs. "It was an accident."

"What about you?" I ask Paisley. "Can you get the cat?"

She pushes her glasses up her nose. "For some reason, Finn Fable runs from me."

"Some reason?" Sophia snorts. "You wanted to shave him for genetic testing."

"I don't know what the big deal is. I merely wanted a small amount of his fur."

I point to Sophia. "What about you?"

She taps her nose. "Allergic."

I open my mouth to ask Maya but she yelps and disappears behind Paisley before I get the chance.

"She's shy," Sophia says.

Chloe smirks. "Except when it comes to Caleb."

I frown. Caleb? As in Caleb Emerson who we went to high school with?

"Those communications are in writing. It's not the same as being in a person's presence," Paisley says.

We're getting sidetracked. I just want someone to get the damn cat for me. I glance around the room and no one will meet my gaze. Shit. I guess it's up to me.

"Where is the cat?"

They answer all at once.

"His litter box is in the laundry room."

"He has a climbing thing in the living room."

"His basket is in Nova's office."

I'll start in the laundry room. There's no cat to be found anywhere near the litter box. But I do find the cat carrier. I grab it and continue my search.

The cat isn't in the living room. Or in Nova's office.

I dig out my phone and message Nova.

> **Is it possible Finn's outside?**

> **Nova: No! Finn is NOT allowed outside. The dog next door will eat him.**

I stuff my phone in my pocket and glance around the living room. The cat has to be here somewhere. Is he hiding?

I get to my knees to search underneath her couch. Sure enough. There's a gray ball of fur in the corner.

"Come on, kitty. Time to go."

Finn hisses at me.

"Don't make me come after you."

I reach an arm under the sofa for him and he scratches me. I yank my arm back and notice he drew blood.

Coaxing the cat out is not going to work. I get to my feet. I can lift the sofa and the cat will be forced out of his hiding place.

I lift the sofa and the cat darts out. I drop the sofa to catch him. But the little shit is fast. He dashes past me and down the hall. I chase after him.

"Don't worry," Sophia says as I pass her. "I'm recording everything for Nova."

I ignore her. I forgot what troublemakers Nova's friends are. The five of them were always getting in trouble in high school. By the looks of it, they haven't stopped causing trouble since then.

I follow the cat into Nova's office.

"Where are you going to hide now? There's no sofa in here."

But there is a desk. The cat scrambles underneath it. There's a problem with his plan. I can easily reach underneath the desk.

Which is what I do. And I receive another scratch for my troubles.

The cat races from the office to Nova's bedroom. I follow him but come to a stop when I notice Maya cradling the cat in her arms.

"He's just scared," she whispers.

"I'll get the cat carrier."

I return to the bedroom with the carrier and the cat goes nuts. Nova could have warned me her cat is fucking crazy.

"I can't hold him," Maya says as she tries to keep control of the cat without getting scratched. Damn. I can't let her get harmed.

I reach over and grab the cat from her. I try to shove him into the carrier but he widens his arms and legs to stop me. Damnit. What now?

"Put him down your shirt," Paisley says.

"I'm not putting a hissing, scratching cat down my shirt."

"It's the best way to calm him down. Your heartbeat will reassure him."

"Go ahead," Chloe urges. "If Paisley says it, it's true."

I've got nothing to lose. Except a nipple. I pull my shirt out, and Finn crawls inside without any prompting.

With a cat in my t-shirt, I carry Nova's suitcases to my truck. Her friends help and soon enough I'm on my way back to the resort.

"You better not scratch, Nova," I tell the cat as we drive. "She's pregnant. If you hurt her, you're going to disappear."

He meows in response. I interpret his meow as agreement.

When I park in front of my chalet, Nova comes rushing out. She yanks my door open. "Is Finn Fable okay?"

I haul the cat out from underneath my t-shirt and hand him to her. He doesn't hiss at her. She cuddles him to her chest. I shake my head. Of course, Nova has a cat that hates everyone except her.

She gasps and I scan the area for any threats. There's no one here.

"You're bleeding."

I glance down at my arms. The bleeding has stopped but there are streaks of blood on my arms.

"Come." Nova shackles my wrist and pulls me toward the chalet. I allow her. "I'll get you cleaned up."

"I can do it."

She rolls her eyes. "No playing the big, bad grouchypants with me. It's my fault you're injured and bleeding. I'll take care of you."

"I'm not injured."

She frowns. "I decide when you're injured."

She drags me into the bathroom. "Sit." When I hesitate, she pushes me onto the closed toilet. "Where are your first aid supplies? Never mind. You sit there. I'll find them."

I like this side of Nova. My cock twitches in agreement. It thinks she's sexy when she's bossy. In all honesty, it finds everything about Nova sexy. It's a bit obsessed with her.

As am I. I shove those thoughts away. I can't be obsessed with Nova since I can't keep her.

Chapter 17

Poker – an excuse to spend time with the people you consider family

Nova

"Have a good evening." I wave to Hudson as I aim for the door.

"Where are you going?"

"It's family night."

"Family night?"

"Drunk poker."

He growls. "You are not drinking."

I roll my eyes and pat my still flat stomach. "Obviously not. I'll be home in a few hours. I'll eat at Sophia's mom's house."

"Hold on." Hudson pushes to his feet. "I need five seconds to change."

"To change? You don't need to come."

"What?"

"You don't need to come."

Hudson has hardly left me alone since he moved me into his chalet. He drives me to work each morning and picks me up at the end of the day, he cooks for me, he lets me watch whatever I want on the television, and—

It's too much! I'm going to declare my undying love to him if he doesn't cut it out.

"What did you say?"

"You don't need to come," I repeat.

He scowls. "Do we need to have the talk again?"

"What talk?"

"The one where I explain how I'm going to take care of you."

I long to hear him say those words about me and only me. Not the me who's carrying his baby. I force those thoughts away. I may be falling in love with Hudson, but he doesn't feel the same way about me. I'm the baby mamma to him and nothing more.

"Stop it." He tucks a strand of hair behind my ear and I startle. I didn't notice him approach while I was off in la-la land dreaming of a place where Hudson loves me for me.

"Stop what?"

He taps my forehead. "Whatever you're thinking that has your brow wrinkling."

Curse the smugglers. He's not supposed to notice when I'm upset. Can't he be the same as every other man I've ever known and pretend to not notice?

"Am I not allowed to think?" I sass since I'm not telling him what I was thinking. No way. No how. I'll allow the pirates to steal me away first.

"You're allowed to think whatever you want. But you're not allowed to be sad about it."

"I'm not allowed to be sad?"

He grunts. "Stop fighting me to fight me."

I don't enjoy how intuitive he is. Hudson is supposed to be the big, bad football player who doesn't have any feelings and is one step up from a hermit. He's not supposed to worry if I'm sad and make me fall for him.

"We're going to be late."

He snatches his keys. "Let's go."

"Don't you want to change first?"

"And give you the chance to run away? Not happening."

"I wouldn't run away."

He cocks an eyebrow.

"I'd drive away."

He grunts but he can't hide from me. I saw the way his lips tipped up. He thinks I'm funny. He just doesn't want to admit it for some reason.

He places a hand on my lower back and I lock my muscles before I shiver at the feel of his oversized, warm hand on me. Too bad my skin is covered. What I wouldn't do to feel his hands all over me again.

He leads me to the passenger side of his truck. He opens the door and before I have a chance to climb in, he lifts me and sets me on the seat.

I should probably protest. But I don't. I love feeling his hands on me in any capacity I can get them. I'm in so much trouble.

Living with Hudson for seven months while I grow this baby is going to end in heartbreak.

I place my hand over my stomach. But I'll have the best consolation prize in the universe. My baby. My family. My future. I can't wait.

"Where are we going?" Hudson asks once we're driving away from the resort toward the town of Smuggler's Rest.

"Lily and Jack's house."

"Sophia and Weston's parents?"

"Lily has the family over once a month. She tried doing Sunday dinners but people would cancel. No one cancels for drunk poker night. And before you say anything, Lily and Jack are my family."

He reaches across the console to squeeze my thigh. "I wasn't going to say anything. I'm glad you had them when your mother passed away."

I sigh. "Lily and Jack are the best. Have you ever heard the story of how they fell in love?"

He shakes his head.

"Jack isn't a native Smuggler. He arrived on the island one summer to do some construction work. He took one look at Lily and was smitten," I begin.

"And there you have it. The story of how Lily and Jack fell in love," I conclude as Hudson parks in front of their house.

Maya's the romantic amongst my group of friends but I appreciate a good love story as much as the next person. I watch Hudson as he rushes around the truck. I blow out a breath.

Unfortunately, I don't believe the 'love' story of Nova and Hudson is going to end in a happily ever after.

Hudson lifts me out of the truck and sets me on my feet.

"You're not going to be able to lift me much longer." I rub my belly. "Once Sprog starts to grow."

He crowds me until my back hits the side of the truck. "You don't think I'm strong enough?"

"Um…" With his heat surrounding me and his sandalwood scent filling the air, I can't remember the question. I want to lean into him. I want to feel his arms around me, surrounding me. I want his lips on mine, exploring my mouth. Filling me with his taste.

"No making out in the driveway!" Sophia shouts from the front door.

"You're cheating. I bet five bucks Hudson couldn't keep his hands off of her," Weston complains.

"Welcome to family night," I mutter.

Hudson tweaks my nose. "You can't scare me off. I have four brothers, remember?"

We begin walking to the house. "I don't think I've met any of your brothers."

"You'll meet them soon. And then you'll wish you hadn't."

Silly man. I can't wait to meet his family. I would have loved to have siblings growing up. A sister to share the burden of caring for Mom when she was sick. A brother to grieve my dad with.

I force thoughts of what I can never have away and smile up at Hudson.

"They can't be that bad."

"Logan holds the record for most detentions given at Smuggler's Hideaway High School."

I gasp. "You're kidding. Someone stole Sophia's record?"

"Hey, Huddy," Weston greets when we reach the porch.

I glare at him. "His name is Hudson."

Weston chuckles as he holds up his hands in surrender. "Another one bites the dust."

"Why is everyone standing on the porch?" Lily pushes her way between Weston and Sophia and smiles at me. "Oh good, you made it. And you brought Hudson with you." She rakes her gaze over him. "Still as handsome as ever, I see."

"Sweet flower," Jack hollers. "No accosting our guests."

"He's not a guest. He's family since he's with Nova."

"He's not… I mean… We're not… What I'm trying to say is—"

Lily snatches my hand and pulls me into the house before I can figure out how to say Hudson and I aren't together despite the baby growing in my belly.

She throws her arms around me and hugs me tight. "I'm excited. Our first grandchild."

"Hey!" Chloe shouts. "Did you forget about Natalia?"

"Of course not," Lily claims. "I meant our first baby grandchild." She wags a finger at Chloe. "I'm still waiting for you to give Natalia a sibling."

Chloe's eyes widen to the size of saucers. "Um…"

Lucas wraps an arm around her shoulders and draws her close. "We're not in a hurry."

My heart fills with happiness for them. Lucas is the best man for Chloe. He knows she's afraid to have children and he supports her instead of pushing her. It's everything she deserves.

I glance up at Hudson from beneath my lashes. He's everything I deserve and want, but he doesn't want me. He wants this baby I'm carrying. Not me. There's not a happy future for us.

"Who's ready for some poker?" Lily asks.

"I'm ready to kick some ass," Weston replies.

Lily slaps him upside the head. "Language."

"Why? There aren't any kids here."

She points at me. "But there will be soon."

I place a hand over my stomach. Not soon enough for me. I can't wait to meet my baby.

Everyone rushes to the poker table in the dining room. Hudson places his hand on my lower back and leads me to the table where he pulls out a chair for me.

"Hudson, the gentleman, is in the building."

He pushes in the chair. "I'm always in the building."

Chloe slaps Lucas. "Why don't you ever pull out a chair for me?"

"Probably because you'd slap me before giving me a lecture on women's equality."

"Women's equality does not exclude men acting as gentlemen," Paisley says as she sits across from me.

Maya sits next to her and gives me a thumbs-up. I roll my eyes. My romantic-obsessed friend believes this is the kick-off of the Nova and Hudson love story. She's wrong. I wish she was right. But she's not.

Hudson wasn't interested in me until I got pregnant. And I can't forget it either. Not if I want to survive Sprog's birth with my heart intact.

Lily arrives with a tray of drinks.

"Those aren't whisky," Weston points out.

"We're doing non-alcoholic drinks since Nova's pregnant."

"You don't have to change things for me," I protest.

Lily shakes her head. "Don't you know, Nova, I'd do anything for you. Anything you need is there for the asking."

My eyes itch and I sniff before any tears can fall. I fail and one tear escapes.

Hudson growls as he wipes the tear away. "You made Nova cry."

I grasp his wrist. "It's okay. It's a happy tear."

"I don't like it when you cry."

"I promise I'm not sad, Mr. Grumpy."

He studies my face for a moment before nodding and kissing my forehead. "If anyone makes you sad, let me know and we'll leave."

It's a good thing I'm sitting because my knees would have given out if I were standing. Hudson seriously needs to stop being sweet. I'm already falling for him.

But he doesn't feel the same. He's protecting me because I'm carrying his baby.

Which is sweet but not what I need.

My heart squeezes. It knows heartbreak is coming for me.

Chapter 18

Grief – doesn't work on a time schedule

NOVA

I inhale a deep breath and blow it out before entering *Five Fathoms Brewery*. Today is my least favorite day of the year. But I'm not going to let it get me down. Mom would be mad at me if I did. And I hate to let her down.

I open the door to the restaurant and Sophia, Chloe, Paisley, and Maya rush to me. They engulf me in a group hug and my resolve to remain strong dissolves. I allow the tears to fall.

Once I feel I've got myself together, I push away and wipe my eyes.

Maya hands me a tissue. "You didn't have to come in today."

I use the tissue to dry my face. "I know."

My girlfriends are the best. They're always supportive. Whether it's the anniversary of my mother's death or another trip to the hospital because of my hypochondria. It doesn't matter. They're there for me.

"Did you tell Hudson?" Sophia asks.

"Why would I tell him it's the anniversary of my mother's death? I'm merely a human incubator to him."

Paisley pushes her glasses up her nose. "You're not using the term incubator correctly."

"You know what I mean."

Chloe raises her hand. "I don't know what you mean."

Maya scowls. "She means Nova's afraid to take a chance on her relationship with Hudson."

"Hudson and I don't have a relationship. He doesn't want me. He wants this baby." I place my hands over my stomach as if I can protect baby Sprog from my words. I wish Sprog could have two parents who love each other, but it's not to be.

"He stares at you as if you hang the moon each night," Maya claims.

I roll my eyes. "You've been reading too many romance novels again."

She sighs. "I do love a grumpy hero."

"Especially if the grumpy hero happens to resemble Hudson. Hubba hubba." Chloe waggles her eyebrows.

I wag my finger at her. "Don't let Lucas hear you drooling over another man."

She grins. "Lucas doesn't mind."

Sophia giggles. "He does mind but you enjoy it when he punishes you."

Chloe doesn't deny it and, despite myself, I'm intrigued.

Maya clasps my hand. "What do you want to do today? Anything you want, we'll do. Mermaid midget golf, *Mermaid Mystical Gardens*, boardwalk, beach. You name it."

I squeeze her hand. "It's sweet but I think I prefer to be alone."

She frowns. "Why did you come into work then?"

"Because she didn't want to tell Hudson about today," Paisley guesses.

Sometimes it's really annoying having a smart friend.

"If you're not ready to tell Hudson, you don't have to," Maya says. She hands me her car keys. "But please don't speed, and make sure to avoid Sammy."

I accept her keys. "How can I avoid Sammy? The seal goes where he wants."

"You could download the Sammy spotting app."

I roll my eyes. "I'm a Smuggler. The app is for tourists."

Since Sammy has become a celebrity due to videos tourists have posted online, the local tourist board developed an app for him. Tourists can add in sightings of the seal, but most tourists use the app to find Sammy.

"At least promise you won't run him over."

I gasp and clutch her keys to my chest. "I would never run Sammy over."

"I don't like this," Paisley declares. "Nova shouldn't be alone today."

"Thank you for your support, Paisley, but I want to be alone."

"It doesn't mean you should be alone."

"I promise I'll be back in a few hours. I just need…"

I trail off. I don't know what I need. It's been more than a decade since Mom passed away but on each anniversary of her death, my grief feels fresh. I've learned to live without her but the pain of the loss is especially sharp today.

Maya hugs me. "Go. We'll be here if you need us."

I suck in a breath to keep the tears welling in my eyes from falling and step out of her arms. "Thanks."

I wave as I exit the brewery. Maya's car is parked in one of the owner's spots. I beep the doors unlocked but before I can get inside, the door to the brewery flies open.

"If you're gone for more than four hours, we're coming after you." Maya doesn't give me a chance to respond before going back inside.

I'm not surprised she gave me an ultimatum. There are limits to my friends' patience. I switch on the engine and back out of the spot. When I turn around, I notice all four of my friends are standing at the front window watching me.

Four hours? I'll be lucky if I get two before they send out a search party. In the previous years, they've dragged me to the *Rumrunner* for shots of whiskey. But not this year. This year I have little Sprog.

Sprog. A child my mom will never meet. She'll never meet her grandchild. Tears flow down my cheeks and I let them. I know from experience there's no stopping the grief on the anniversary of her death.

I drive aimlessly around the island for a while until I find myself in front of the cemetery. I'm not surprised I'm here. I visit Mom and Dad at least four times a year, if not more.

Guilt swamps me when I realize I haven't visited since my night with Hudson over two months ago. I hop out of the car and make my way to the flower shop next door where I buy a bouquet of pink tulips for Mom and a bunch of wildflowers for Dad.

Mom loved tulips. Dad bought her a bouquet at least once a month. But there was no schedule as to when he'd come home to surprise her with her favorite flowers or a box of fancy chocolate.

They were deeply, madly in love. I want what they had. Even if I can only have it for a short time like they did. I don't want to compromise and be with someone who's only interested in me because I'm having his baby. It doesn't matter if I'm falling for him. A one-sided relationship is certain to bring misery.

I carry my flowers into the cemetery and wander the paths until I reach their graves. Leo Myers and Stella Myers.

I sweep some debris from their graves before leaning the flowers against their headstones. I sit on the grass in between them.

"Hi, Mom. Hi, Dad."

Thirteen years. I can't believe it's been thirteen years since I last saw my mom. Another eleven years on top of those since I saw Dad. I miss them so much.

"Sorry it's been a while."

I pluck on the grass while I try to figure out a way to tell them what's happening.

"I'm having a baby," I blurt out. "And, no, I'm not married." I clear my throat. "Actually, I'm not in a relationship with the father's baby. It's Hudson by the way. You remember Hudson

Clark? Big football star in high school who went on to be a professional in the NFL. He ruptured his Achilles' tendon a few years back and came home."

"I feel bad for him. It must be horrible to watch your dreams go up in flames. Although, he's not doing too bad now. He established this super luxurious resort on the other side of the island. You should see the chalets. They're to die for. With plunge pools on the terraces. You know how much I love pools."

I realize I'm rambling and pause.

"It was a one-night stand. I know. I know. I shouldn't have given into temptation but have you seen Hudson? The man is a walking, talking wet dream." I cringe. "Sorry, Dad."

"How do I feel about him?" My smile is wistful. "I think I'm falling in love with him."

"I wish you were here to talk to. I wish I could ask you how it feels to fall in love. I wish I could hear you tell me the story of how you met one more time."

Too many wishes that will never be fulfilled.

I realize I'm crying and wipe my eyes with my sleeve.

"We won't be a family in the traditional sense but I will have a family. The baby I've always wanted. I wish Sprog could meet you. You'd be the best grandparents in the world. You'd spoil him rotten and I'd have to be the mean mom every time he came home from visiting you."

"Nova!"

I glance over my shoulder. Hudson is barreling down the path toward me.

"What are you doing here?"

Chapter 19

Holding – when Hudson realizes he's feeling possessive about the mother of his child

HUDSON

I frown when the phone rings and rings. Why isn't Nova answering? She seemed sad this morning but when I asked her what was wrong, she merely shrugged.

I'm worried she's not feeling well. She tries not to tell me when she's sick since she's afraid I'll judge her for being a hypochondriac. She's growing my baby. I would never judge her.

I thought I'd make a special dinner to cheer her up but I wanted to check what time she'll be finished with work. Thus, the phone call. But she's not answering.

I hang up and dial her extension at the brewery. No answer.

Now, I'm getting worried. Is she at the hospital? She'd tell me if she went to the hospital, wouldn't she?

I pace my office for a few minutes as I contemplate what to do. I can drive to the brewery to check on her. The *Five Fathoms Brewing* restaurant has the best burgers in town. I could say I had a craving. Nova wouldn't know I was there to check on her.

It's not yet noon but I'm not waiting any longer. I grab my keys and hurry toward the parking lot. My phone rings before I reach my truck.

Relief pours through me. Nova's okay. There's nothing wrong. But when I check the screen of my phone it's not Nova calling.

"Where's Nova?" I ask Maya.

"Um…"

I realize I barked out my question and try to soften my voice for Nova's shy friend. "Maya, where's Nova?"

"I don't know."

My heart races and fear fills me. "You don't know? Isn't she working with you?"

"We gave her four hours to be alone but it's been three and no one knows where she is. Lucas and Weston have been searching the island but no one's seen her."

I stop in front of my truck. "Hold on. Start over. Why did you give her four hours to be alone?"

"I'm not supposed to tell," she whispers.

"I think it's too late for secrets, Maya."

"She's going to kill me."

"Maya, I need to find Nova. Please help me."

She blows out a breath. "Today is the anniversary of the day Nova's mom died."

Fuck! And she didn't tell me. I knew there was something wrong. My sunshine's light was dimmed today. And I'm the asshole who let her go to work when it was obvious she was upset.

"And you let her go off on her own!"

"It's an island. Where could she go?"

"Not far since she's on foot."

"Um…"

I growl. "Out with it."

"She has my car."

My nostrils flare and I inhale a deep breath before I yell at Maya. This is not her fault. It's mine. I knew something was off with Nova this morning and I let it go.

"Message me the make and model of the car as well as the license plate. I'm getting in my truck now."

"I'm sorry, Hudson. I thought I was doing the right thing."

I blow out a breath. "It's okay, Maya. Let's concentrate on finding Nova for now."

"I'll message you," she says and rings off.

As soon as the call disconnects, I dial Weston. While the phone rings, I switch on my truck and start driving out of the parking lot.

"Huddy," Weston answers.

I ignore the childish nickname. "Where am I driving?"

"Are you out searching for Nova?"

"Why is this a question? Of course, I'm searching for Nova. Where have you searched?"

"You care for her."

I growl. "Of course, I care for her. It's Nova. Enough with the stupid questions. What direction should I drive in?"

He clears his throat. "Lucas is covering Smuggler's Rest and I'm on my way to Rogue's Landing."

There's only one other town on the island. "I've got Pirate's Perch."

"Let us know if you find her."

I grunt and hang up.

I turn left toward Pirate's Perch and start speeding down the road. I need to find Nova. I can't stand the idea of her somewhere all alone grieving her mom.

Grieving her mom? Of course. That's it. I know where she is. I do a U-turn and head back toward Smuggler's Rest. There's one cemetery on the island and it's in Smuggler's Rest.

I screech into the parking lot and search the area for Maya's car. There. It's here. I feel as if I can breathe for the first time today. Nova's here. She's safe.

But the urge to find her, to hold her in my arms, to comfort her still pounds through my veins. I jump out of my truck and rush through the cemetery.

When I finally spot her, I shout her name, "Nova!"

She glances over her shoulder and the devastation on her face nearly causes me to stumble. My sunshine should never be sad.

"What are you doing here?"

I don't answer her question. I fall to my knees and haul her into my arms. She doesn't protest. She melts into my hold. She hiccups and I realize she's crying again.

I hold her while she cries. Until my shirt is soaked with her tears. When she's quiet, I pinch her chin to lift her face. Her eyes are puffy and her nose is red.

"I'm sorry."

I scowl. "What are you sorry for?"

She huffs. "For being a mess. I promise I'll be happy tomorrow."

"Don't do that."

"Do what?"

"Act as if you're happy when you're not."

She smiles at me. "I am happy. Most of the time at least. I promised Mom I wouldn't let her death cause me to live in sorrow. And I haven't."

She's amazing. She suffered more grief in her teenage years than most people suffer in their entire lives and yet she's happy and smiling and my sunshine. No wonder I'm falling in love with her.

The realization doesn't surprise me. I've always wanted Nova. When we were in high school and she was an adorable teenager who got blackballed from the cheerleading squad, I wanted her. Since I've returned to the island, I've wanted her.

I'll always want Nova. She's the light to my darkness.

"Do you want to sit a little while longer with your parents?" She grins up at me. "There's my sunshine."

"Do you want to meet them?"

I nod.

Her grin widens. "Mom, Dad, this is Hudson."

I don't know what to say but the problem is solved for me by Nova when she starts babbling to the graves of her parents.

"He's my baby daddy. You remember him from high school. Don't say anything, Mom. He doesn't need to know how I crushed on him in high school."

I chuckle and Nova gasps.

"You laughed."

I scowl. "I didn't laugh."

"I heard you." She stands and wipes the dirt and grass from her clothes. "Bye, Mom and Dad. I'll see you soon."

I clasp her hand and lead her toward the exit. Her hand is small compared to mine but it feels right walking with her and holding her hand.

This is the woman for me. I don't want to dim her sunshine with my grumpiness but considering what she's been through and how she still smiles and lights up a room with her sunshine, I'm no longer worried about darkening her light.

"Are you feeling better?"

She bobs her head. "I am. The anniversary of Mom's death is always sad, but I'm glad I got a chance to visit with her."

"Do you come to the cemetery often?"

"A few times a year." She pauses. "How did you find me here anyway? Wait. Did Maya send you?"

"Whole town is looking for you."

She groans. "The whole town?"

I tuck a strand of hair behind her ear. I want to touch more than her face but I need to be patient. Except for our one night together, Nova's made it clear she doesn't want me. I'll change her mind. But I need time.

I drop my hand. "They love you. They care for you. They worry about you." They're not the only ones.

"I'm never going to hear the end of this."

"If anyone gives you a hard time, let me know. I'll handle them."

She giggles. "The big bad grump is going to handle it."

She thinks I'm joking. I'm not. I won't allow anyone to hurt Nova. She's mine to protect.

Chapter 20

Hellions – four brothers who can't wait to be uncles

Nova

I wring my hands in my lap as Hudson drives us toward his parents' house.

"There's no need to be nervous." He reaches across the console to squeeze my hand. "My parents are going to love you."

I hope he's right since his parents are the sole grandparents our little Sprog will have. I want to have a good relationship with them. I want them to spend time with our baby and me. Not avoid me because they hate me.

"I hope your mom likes the flowers."

"She's going to love the flowers. She has five boys. She doesn't get flowers very often."

"Your dad doesn't buy her flowers? My dad bought my mom flowers all the time. My parents were such an adorable couple."

I sigh. I want to be half of an adorable couple. I glance over at Hudson from beneath my lashes. I want to be an adorable couple with him. I shove those fantasies away. Now is not the time to lament falling in love with my baby daddy who doesn't want me. Now is the time to freak out about meeting his parents.

"We're here." Hudson parks in front of a ranch house. Several cars are blocking the driveway as well as a few bikes laying on their sides in the front lawn. It appears crowded and homey.

He opens my door and lifts me out of the truck onto the ground. He intertwines his fingers with mine as he leads me to the front door. I cling to his hand.

The front door flies open and a young man steps outside. "They're here!"

"Brace yourself," Hudson mutters.

"Brace myself? Why do I need to brace myself? You said they'd like me."

My heart hammers in my chest and I wonder how fast I can run away. I knew I should have driven my own car. But I haven't driven my car since I've been living with Hudson. He growls whenever I pick up my car keys. Is it wrong to enjoy how much he prefers to drive me around?

"My brothers are hellions."

"Is this her?" the young man on the step asks. Three more boys appear behind him.

Holy smugglers. They're all tall and have Hudson's brown eyes and brown hair. If it weren't for their age differences, they could be quintuplets.

"Stop barring the front door and let them in." A middle-aged woman pushes her way in between the boys. She's tiny compared to the rest of them, but she shares their brown eyes.

"Mom." Hudson greets her with a kiss on the cheek. "This is Nova."

I smile at her. "It's nice to meet you, Mrs. Clark. I brought you these." I shove the pink tulips into her hands. "My mom loved tulips. I thought you might like them as well. Hudson says your boys don't bring you flowers."

Mrs. Clark giggles. "Since we're family now, you can call me Emma."

Family now? My hand automatically reaches for my stomach. "I didn't mean to get pregnant. It was an accident."

Emma winks. "We know all about accidents in this family." She glares at her boys. "But we use protection to prevent accidents as much as possible."

One of the boys rolls his eyes. "Yes, Mom. We use condoms."

Hudson slaps his shoulder. "Knock off the sarcasm."

Emma motions us further into the house. "Come inside where you can properly meet my boys."

"Hellions," Hudson mutters underneath his breath.

"This is Brooks." She points to the sarcastic boy. "And this is Logan, Owen, and Sawyer."

"Your baby mamma is hot."

Owen barely gets the words out before Hudson smacks him on the head. He falls forward and lands on his knees. He bursts into laughter as he rolls around on the floor.

"Boys," a man grumbles as he enters the living room.

I stick out my hand. "You must be Mr. Clark. I was going to bring you flowers, too, but Hudson said flowers are for women.

He's wrong but I didn't want to fight with him. I know how to pick my battles and flowers are not a hill I'm willing to die on."

Mr. Clark chuckles as he shakes my hand. "She's cute, Hudson."

Hudson wraps an arm around my shoulders and hauls me near. "She is."

What is he doing? Do his parents think we're a couple? Oh no. I'm not prepared. Hudson didn't warn me. I'm going to kill him later. A former football player can totally drown in his bathtub without it appearing suspicious, right?

"And she's freaking out," Logan says.

I gasp. "You're not supposed to mention if I'm freaking out."

His cheeks darken. "Sorry. I didn't know."

"Logan's a nerd. He doesn't understand social cues'." Owen uses air quotes as if social cues is a made up term. "He prefers to stay home and study rather than go out."

Sawyer snorts. "Not everyone enjoys jumping out of their bedroom window."

Owen shrugs. "It's the first floor. No big deal."

Emma clears her throat. "Can you all please calm down? I don't want Nova to think she's bringing a child into a clan of cave bears."

"Don't worry," I say. "I'm used to the grumpy bear here."

Sawyer barks out a laugh. "She's got you pegged."

Hudson growls at him. "Behave."

"Or what?"

"Or I'll tell everyone how you refused to be potty trained until second grade."

Sawyer glares at his older brother. "You suck."

"According to his girlfriend, he doesn't know how to suck." Brooks waggles his eyebrows. "If you know what I mean."

"Don't talk about my girlfriend." Sawyer launches himself at Brooks and the two fall to the floor where they roll around while trying to get hits in.

I elbow Hudson. "Aren't you going to stop them?"

He shrugs. "They'll stop soon enough."

I narrow my eyes on him. "Is this the kind of dad you're going to be? You're going to allow our Sprog to get into fights. Great. I'll have to be the bad guy who disciplines Sprog. Thanks a lot. You know how I hate to be the bad guy."

"Hold on. Sprog?" Emma asks. "Do you know the sex of the baby? Is it a boy? I swear the Clark men can't create girls. But I want a little girl to spoil."

"Um… we don't know the sex of the baby. It's too early. Although the doctor said we can find out at our next appointment."

She crosses her fingers. "Please be a girl. Please be a girl."

"You're not annoyed I got pregnant after a one-night stand with your son?" My eyes widen when I realize what I said. Holy Neptune! I just admitted to having a one-night stand to Hudson's mom.

Emma bursts into laughter. "Annoyed? I'm relieved Hudson's the first son to give me a grandchild." She thumbs her finger at Brooks. "I was sure this one would be the first and he's still in high school."

Hudson squeezes my shoulder. "I told you they wouldn't care."

Mr. Clark throws an arm around his wife. "I'd be a hypocrite if I was mad since I got her pregnant in high school." He glares at his four younger sons. "But I expect the lot of you to learn from my mistakes."

Logan removes his glasses and cleans them with his t-shirt. "Can we please have one conversation in this house that doesn't involve coitus?"

"Coitus?" Owen snorts. "No wonder you never get any."

"Perhaps I'm waiting for someone special instead of fornicating with every girl in school."

"I don't know if I want your brothers babysitting our baby," I say.

"I warned you," Hudson mutters.

"You couldn't have expected me to believe you. You barely speak, but your brothers are all motor mouths with smooth lines and troublemaker written all over them."

"Hudson was our responsible child." Mr. Clark scowls at his other sons. "Whereas the rest of our sons are hellions."

"I am not a hellion," Logan declares.

Mr. Clark rolls his eyes. "He thinks because he uses scientific experiments to cause trouble, he's not a hellion. He's wrong."

"He reminds me of Paisley."

"Who's Paisley?" Logan asks.

"She's the brewer of *Five Fathoms Brewing*. We own the brewery together with three other friends."

"You own *Five Fathoms Brewing*?" Brooks asks.

I wag my finger at him. "I am not allowing you to drink underage."

"Damn."

"No cussing," Emma admonishes. "I swear I did my best to raise them. I promise I'll be a good grandmother to your little one. You have no need to worry."

My mouth drops open. "Are you seriously concerned I won't want you to be around your grandchild?"

Her cheeks darken and she shrugs.

I rush forward to grasp her hands. "I want you around our little Sprog. I want him or her to have a grandmother. I'm relying on you to be their family since I don't have any."

Her eyes well with tears but she sniffs to stop them from falling. "Thank you, Nova. I'll be the best grandmother you could ever imagine."

"I'm certain you will. But just in case, I hope Sprog's a girl." I wink to let her know I'm joking.

"I like her," she declares. "You chose well, Hudson, my boy."

I step back. "Oh, we're not… um… together." The words burn as I say them. I want to be with Hudson. I want to be part of his crazy, rambunctious family. Now I'm the one fighting tears. "I'll never deny him access to his child, but we're not a family."

Hudson wraps his arm around my waist. "We are a family. We're not a traditional family. But we're a family."

My heart spasms in my chest as I force myself to smile at him. I wish his words were true. But they're not.

Chapter 21

Offside – when a baby is not positioned where it's supposed to be

HUDSON

"Nova! Come on. We're going to be late."

I prowl the living room as I wait for her to come out of her bedroom. I hate her having a separate bedroom. I want her in *my* bedroom. In *my* bed. With me. I want to hold her in my arms all night long every night.

And she will be in my bedroom. I won't allow for anything else.

"What's the hurry?" Nova asks as she rushes into the living room.

"It's my first doctor appointment. I don't want to be late."

Her smile lights up the room. "You're excited about the doctor's appointment?"

"Hell, yeah, I am. Today is the mid-pregnancy ultrasound. We can hear Sprog's heartbeat and find out their gender."

She freezes. "Find out the gender?"

"Do you not want to know if Sprog is a girl or a boy?"

Her nose wrinkles in that adorable way it does when she's unsure. "I don't know."

"Let's discuss this on the way. I don't want to be late."

She giggles. "I never thought Mr. Crabby Crabapple would be worried about being late."

I never used to be. Until I arrived late at football practice once when I was a senior because I couldn't get Brooks ready for school on time. After spending an hour running laps around the field, I decided to never be late again.

I usher Nova out of the chalet and into my truck. Warmth spreads through me when she allows me to lift her up into the passenger seat. She smiles at me and I can't resist her. I kiss her forehead before clicking her seatbelt into place.

I'm not a man who needs a woman to follow his rules but I do want a woman who allows me to care for her the way Nova does. Or maybe I just want Nova. She's all I can see and hear.

"I want to know the gender of the baby," I announce once we're driving toward the hospital where the OB/GYN has her practice.

"You couldn't have mentioned this before today?"

"Sorry. I thought after you and my mom oohed and aahed over having a girl you wanted to know."

"Are you okay with having a girl?"

I glance over at her. "Why wouldn't I be okay with a girl?"

She shrugs and glances out of the window to avoid my gaze. "You're a manly man. You have four brothers. Girls don't seem to fit into your life."

I grasp her hand. "You fit into my life."

She snorts. "Because you knocked me up."

"Best mistake of my life."

She gasps. "Are you serious?"

I grunt. I don't want to explain how spending a night tangled up in the sheets with her was the single most sexy experience of my life. Or how her getting pregnant allowed me to see past my fear of ruining her. Or how I'm falling in love with her.

She rubs a hand over her belly. Her pregnancy is still not visible but every time she touches her stomach and reminds me of the child we created, I get hard. My cock twitches and I clear my throat before I get hard now.

She rolls her eyes. "A grunt is not an answer."

"We're here," I announce instead of responding to her.

I park and help her out of my truck. I enjoy the feeling of her in my arms. It's why I often carry her out of the truck. I want her in my arms where I can protect her and cherish her as often as possible.

"You ready?" I ask as I lace my fingers with hers and lead her into the hospital.

She bounces on her toes. "Beyond ready. I can't wait to hear Sprog's heartbeat and see the little fingers and toes."

Her smile spreads from ear to ear and her eyes sparkle with happiness. Those dark, exotic eyes mesmerize me. I want to stare into them while I'm moving inside of her, buried deep.

So much for not getting hard this morning.

"Nova Myers," Nova announces to the receptionist and I scowl. Nova's last name should be the same as mine – Clark.

But we're not there. She doesn't even realize we're a couple yet.

"Have a seat," the receptionist says and I place my hand on Nova's lower back to guide her to a chair.

I notice several women staring at me as we settle in our seats but I ignore them – the only woman I'm interested in is sitting next to me – and pull out my phone to check my email while we wait.

"Psst," Nova whispers.

I grunt since I'm in the middle of reading an email about some water damage to one of our chalets.

"Psst."

When I don't respond this time, she elbows me. I set my phone down.

"What is it?"

"Keep it down," she whispers.

"What is it?" I mumble.

"All the women here are staring at you."

I don't bother scanning the room to confirm. I don't care.

"So?"

"So?"

"Yeah. So?"

"They're practically drooling over you."

"They're not drooling over me." I learned long ago the attention has nothing to do with me. It's about the fame being a football player brought me. They want to feel the attention if only for a second.

She giggles. "I beg to differ."

I grasp her hand. "I'm not interested in anyone other than you."

She rolls her eyes. "Because I'm your baby mamma."

She's a lot more than my baby mamma. She's the woman I want to spend my days and nights with. She's the woman I want to build a family with. She's the woman I want. Period.

"Nova Myers," a nurse calls before I have a chance to answer. Which is probably for the better. A hospital waiting room is not the appropriate place to reveal to Nova that our relationship has changed.

We follow the nurse into a room. "Dr. Katz will be with you in a moment," she says before leaving us.

Nova picks up the gown and hurries behind the curtain to change. I settle into a chair next to the exam table.

"Not a word," she orders before coming out from behind the curtain wearing the hospital gown and a pair of fuzzy socks.

"You look adorable," I say as I help her onto the exam table. I kiss her nose before sitting down again.

"Adorable?" She snorts. "I don't think you know the meaning of the word."

The door opens and the doctor rushes in. "Nova." Her brow wrinkles when she realizes Nova isn't alone. "Who is this?" Her gaze rakes up and down me.

"This is Hudson. Hudson this is Dr. Katz."

"Is Hudson your baby daddy?"

Nova's cheeks heat but she nods.

"No wonder you got pregnant the first time the two of you had sex."

I chuckle.

Nova gasps. "You laughed."

My brow wrinkles. "I laugh."

She rolls her eyes. "Not very often, tallest crab apple in the orchard."

Dr. Katz laughs. "You two are adorable. I love it when my adorable couples have babies."

"We're not a—"

I squeeze Nova's hand to cut her off. "We're excited about today's scan."

The doctor settles on a stool next to the ultrasound machine. "Do you want to know the sex of the baby?"

Nova raises an eyebrow at me.

"I do. Nova isn't sure yet."

"If you want to know, we'll find out," Nova says.

"You don't have to do that."

"Do what?"

"Allow my wants to trump yours. Your wants are just as valid as mine."

Dr. Katz sighs. "I love the caring baby daddies. They're the best."

"I think our doctor has love on the brain," Nova whispers to me. "She should join Maya's book club."

"Well," the doctor prompts. "Yes, to the baby's gender?"

"Lady's choice," I say.

Nova nibbles on her lip and I fist my hand before I reach forward to free her lip from her teeth. It's not my place. Not yet.

"Okay," she breathes out.

I smile. "Okay?"

"You're smiling. Definitely the right decision."

"Here we go." The doctor lifts up Nova's gown to reveal her belly. It's still mostly flat since she hasn't 'popped' yet.

I'm fascinated by the sight of her naked skin. I squeeze Nova's hand to stop myself from touching her. Now is not the time. Soon, though. I hope.

"This is going to be cold." The doctor squeezes gel onto Nova's belly and Nova gasps. "Sorry."

The doctor places the probe on her belly and glides it around. "Before I determine the sex, I'll check the baby's health."

"Baby Sprog is okay, isn't he?"

"We'll find out now," Dr. Katz reassures Nova.

I push Nova's hair off of her forehead. "I'm sure the baby's fine. And, if not, we'll deal with it."

"You're always calm."

"It helps to remain calm when a three-hundred-pound defense lineman is barreling his way down the field at you."

"I knew it! You're Double Crown. I'm delivering Double Crown's baby." The doctor appears excited about the idea.

"It's Nova's baby, too," I point out.

She clears her throat. "Of course." The doctor glides the probe over Nova's belly. "Look here." She points to the screen. "Here are the baby's fingers. Five on each hand." She glides the probe to a different location. "And here are the feet. Let me count the toes. Five on each foot. The baby is looking good. Do you want to hear the heart?"

Nova's eyes light up with excitement. "Yes, please."

The doctor flips a switch on the machine and the room fills with the whoosh-whoosh sound of our baby's heartbeat.

Nova squeezes my hand. "It's Sprog. Our baby."

A tear leaks from her eye and I wipe it away. "Our baby."

Excitement and wonder fill me. We made this tiny creature. I can't wait to meet him or her. I really don't care what the gender of the baby is, but I know Nova wants a girl. She hasn't said she does but the way she lights up whenever she talks about having a little girl makes her choice obvious. For her sake, I hope it's a girl.

"Now to find out if our little one is a girl or a boy."

Dr. Katz moves the probe around for a while. She frowns as she works.

"Is something wrong?" I ask.

"Sometimes a baby doesn't cooperate when we want to figure out the gender."

"What do you mean?" Nova asks.

"I mean your baby is mooning me and refusing to show me their genitals."

I bark out a laugh. "Our baby is mooning you."

She taps the monitor where it does appear as if the baby is showing us its rear end.

"This is Hudson's fault," Nova declares. "I met his family. Trust me. It's their genes causing our baby to moon you."

"We're all done here," the doctor announces. "I'll print out a picture of the baby and you can schedule your next appointment with the receptionist."

She hands the picture to Nova before standing and snapping her gloves off. She offers me her hand. "Nice to meet you, baby daddy."

I chuckle as I shake her hand. Leave it to my sunshine girl to have an OB/GYN who's amusing.

She leaves and I return my attention to Nova who's clutching the picture to her chest. "We're having a baby," she whispers as tears fall down her face.

"Hey now." I wipe the tears from her face. "There's no reason to cry."

She smiles at me. "I'm feeling too many emotions and they're leaking from my eyes."

"You're nutty, Sunshine."

Nutty or emotional or laughing, I don't mind. I just want this woman in my life forever. Now to convince her she wants to be in mine.

Chapter 22

Surprise – when the man you're falling for gives you everything you want and scares the pants off of you

NOVA

I yawn as we drive down the driveway toward Hudson's chalet.

"Lunch was good but I'm ready for a nap."

Growing a baby is tiring. I can't remember the last time I felt as if I got enough sleep despite sleeping nine hours a night.

I clutch the image from the ultrasound in my hand. I'll accept tired for the rest of my life to hold baby Sprog in my hands.

"Before your nap, I have a surprise for you."

"What surprise?"

He chuckles. "It wouldn't be a surprise if I told you."

"Are you going to show me?" I cross my fingers and raise them in the air. "Please be a pool. Please be a pool."

"You want a pool, I'll get you a pool."

My mouth drops open. "I was joking. You can't snap your fingers and suddenly you have a pool."

"You'd be surprised what I can do with my fingers."

Tingles erupt in my belly and travel to my core where my panties dampen. I wouldn't be surprised. I know exactly what he can do with those fingers. Give me pleasure I've never felt before.

I lift my hand to fan my face but drop it before he notices. Hudson Clark doesn't want me. He wants this baby I'm carrying.

"Is the surprise a massage? I could do with a massage. My back is sore all the time."

He frowns. "You didn't tell me your back is sore. You didn't tell the doctor either."

"I told Dr. Katz at my last appointment. She said it's normal during pregnancy."

"I'll have the masseuse come over this afternoon to give you a massage."

I'm disappointed he doesn't want to give me a massage, but I don't take it personally. It's just more proof he doesn't want me. He wants the baby.

"What's this surprise if it's not a massage?"

"I have to show you." He exits the truck and I wait for him to come around to my side.

"Do you want me to carry you? How sore is your back?"

"I can walk." I don't want to, though. I want him to carry me everywhere.

He ignores my words and lifts me into his arms to carry me to the front door. The door clicks open but he doesn't set me down. He walks down the hallway to the spare bedroom. He sets me on my feet before reaching for the door.

"This is your surprise."

He pushes the door open and I step inside. I expect there to be a gift on the bed, but there's no bed. In fact, all of the furniture from the spare bedroom is gone because this room is now a nursery.

There's a crib in one corner next to a changing table. In the other corner is a rocking chair. And, smack dab in the middle of the room, there's an oversized stuffed seal. It reminds me of Sammy. The walls are covered in wallpaper with scenes from the sea in it, including mermaids and treasure chests.

"It's perfect."

He wraps his arms around me from behind and kisses my hair. "You like it?"

"I love it. The baby will love spending time here when they're with you."

He scowls.

"What? What's wrong?"

He urges me toward the rocking chair. "Sit. We need to talk."

Oh great. It's time for 'the talk'. Does he want me to leave now? Does he want full custody? I clasp my chest. No. He can't have full custody. This baby is mine.

"Hey. Hey." He kneels before me and pulls my hands away from my chest. "What's wrong?"

"You can't have this baby. I won't give Sprog to you."

His brow wrinkles. "What are you talking about?"

I yank my hand from his and motion to the room. "You made this room for the baby. So you can have the baby here all the time. So you can steal the baby from me."

"I do want baby Sprog here all the time."

I gasp. "I knew it! You're stealing my baby. And you're the big, important football hero. What chance do I have to fight you?"

"I don't want you to fight me."

"Tough. I'm fighting you. I'm not giving you my baby."

"I don't want you to give me the baby."

"You do want to fight me?"

He sighs. "Nova, my sunshine, I'm not explaining myself very well."

I snort. "No, you're not, Captain Grumpy."

"I want the baby here because I want you here."

"It's sweet of you to offer for me to live with you but I have a house in Smuggler's Rest. Once the baby is born and you know they're safe, there's no reason for me to live here."

He brushes the hair off of my forehead. "Yes, there is."

When he doesn't say more, I push. "What reason? What are you talking about?"

"I'm talking about you and me. I want us to be a family."

"We are a family. Mom, baby daddy, and baby."

"No. A family as in mom, dad, baby."

My pulse speeds up until I can hear the thump-thump in my ears. "W-w-what?"

"Nova Myers, I want you. Not because you're the mother of my children."

"Child," I correct. "Dr. Katz confirmed I am not having twins."

"I want you to be the mother of all of my children, not just baby Sprog."

I gasp. "What are you saying?"

"I'm saying I like you, Nova. I want our relationship to be real. Not a friendship because we're having a baby together. But a romantic relationship where I get to hold you and kiss you and spend the night wrapped around your body."

"I don't know what I'm more shocked by. How many words you spoke or the words you actually said."

He kisses my nose. "What do you say, Nova? Are you going to put me out of my misery?"

I open my mouth to shout yes! I want you! I want this! But fear grasps hold of me and the words won't come.

Hudson is giving me everything I've ever wanted. He's the man I want. He's the man I've wanted forever. He's the man I'm falling in love with. The man who wants to take care of me. The man who cooks for me. The man who opens the door for me. The man who carries me. The man who built a nursery for our baby.

But what if I give in to him and allow myself to love him? He'll die. Everyone I love dies. It's my curse to bear.

"What's wrong, Sunshine?"

I nibble on my bottom lip but Hudson reaches forward to remove my lip from my teeth. "I know I'm not exactly a catch."

I rear back. "What? You're not a catch? Have you covered up all the mirrors in your bedroom? Or forgotten how you own this successful business? It's been less than two hours since someone reminded you of winning two Super Bowl Championships. What in all of those awesome accomplishments says you're not a catch?"

"Says the woman who refers to me as the King of the Grumps."

"You smiled today. And you laughed. I'm breaking you out of your grumpy persona."

"If anyone can, it's you."

"You're serious?"

"Yes."

"Come on, Sunshine. Give me a chance. I'll make it worth your while."

I know he will. He's everything I've ever wanted. He's offering me the one thing I want. A family. A real family.

But my heart is lodged in my throat and my stomach is filled with dread. What if he dies? I can't handle it if another person in my life who I love dies. I won't survive.

"I don't know."

He frames my face with his hands. "Give me a chance, Nova. I know I've been an ass in the past. Because I was trying to resist you. But you're irresistible. No one can withstand the lure of your sunshine. I certainly couldn't."

He's making it awful hard to say no. Don't say no, my heart whispers.

The temptation is too much to resist. "No promises, but why don't we go out on a date? See how it goes. Maybe you'll change your mind when you realize I can't eat without spilling food down my bra."

He chuckles. "I already know you can't eat without spilling food."

I scowl at him. "You're not supposed to mention it."

He presses his lips to mine but pulls back before I have a chance to wrap my arms around him and enjoy the feel of him touching me.

"Thank you, Sunshine. You won't regret this."

I hope he's right. I hope I'm not making the biggest mistake of my life. I hope this doesn't end in heartbreak. Or, worse yet, tragedy.

Chapter 23

Fumble – when Hudson loses control of the date

HUDSON

I offer Nova my arm. "Are you ready?"

"I'm ready. I just don't know why I had to wear a swimsuit underneath my dress. It's not warm enough to swim in the ocean." She shivers.

"You don't enjoy swimming in the ocean."

Her nose wrinkles. "There are creepy crawlers and things with sharp teeth in the water."

I chuckle as I open the door for her and usher her outside. She heads toward my truck but I steer her in the other direction.

"Is this the part where you lure me into the woods to drink my blood?"

I cough to hide my amusement. "Drink your blood?"

"Maya is on a vampire romance kick."

"Vampires aren't real."

"I know but don't tell Maya. She would be majorly disappointed."

"I promise not to tell Maya vampires don't exist even though they don't."

"If we're not going into the woods for you to suck my blood, where are we going? And is it far? I wore these sandals for our date but I hadn't expected to do much walking."

She kicks up one foot to show me her sandals. The silky straps wrap around her ankles up to her knees. They're sexy as fuck. I'd leave them on while I flipped up her dress and buried myself deep inside her. My cock twitches in agreement.

I blow out a breath. I'm not having sex with Nova tonight. She needs to realize there's more to us than our incredible chemistry in bed.

"These sandals are not made for walking."

"Do you want me to carry you?"

She skids to a stop. "Carry me? You're going to carry me all the way to this mystery place we're going to?"

I shrug. "I blew out my Achilles' tendon but my arms still work."

"Based on the amount of running you do every morning, your Achilles isn't slowing you down any."

Except it ruined my career. What is an athlete when he can't play pro ball? A resort owner, apparently. I scowl. Resort owner was nowhere on my list of career goals.

I shake those thoughts out of my mind. I'm not going to be all melancholy on my date with the woman I'm falling for. She deserves my attention. She deserves everything.

"Do you want me to carry you?"

"Depends. How far are we going?"

"You're not very good at handling surprises, are you?"

She shrugs. "None of my friends are."

"Considering who your friends are, I'm not surprised."

She elbows me. "Hey, don't speak badly about my friends. They're my ride and dies. If you're with me, you're with them."

"I wasn't speaking badly of them. I was merely pointing out how your friends couldn't wait to find out where senior skip day was so they broke into the principal's office to figure it out."

"They should have never teased us about it being the best senior skip day ever. Who can resist the temptation?"

"Not you." I chuckle.

"You laughed. I win!"

I shake my head. Nova is funny. What was I thinking? Avoiding her since I came home three years ago? I've lost three years with my funny sunshine.

We reach the resort chalets furthest from the main building.

"Are we having dinner at the resort restaurant?" Nova asks.

"No."

"But we are going to the resort?"

"Maybe."

She pinches me. "You're no fun."

"Trust me, Sunshine. I'm lots of fun."

Her eyes flare and she licks her bottom lip. I'm tempted to touch those lips. Taste her mouth. Explore every inch of her. But I inhale a deep breath instead.

I want to give Nova a night to remember.

"Shall we?" I motion to the structure behind the main building.

"What's in here?" She doesn't wait for an answer before opening the door and entering. She squeals. "It's a pool!"

"I closed the pool for the night."

"There's no one else coming?"

I motion to the table set up next to the pool in one of the cabanas. "Except for the wait staff."

She hurries to the table and sinks into one of the lounge chairs. She groans as she settles in. "You're going to have to haul me out of this chair after dinner."

"I'll haul you anywhere you want to go."

And I do mean anywhere. Anything Nova wants, she gets. I plan to spoil her rotten. I'm going to get her addicted to me. She won't want to ever leave me. Not that I'm ever going to let her. She leaves me, I'm chasing her down.

I sit across from her and motion to the waitress waiting by the entrance to the pool. She arrives with a bottle of champagne.

Nova holds up her hand. "None for me." She points to her belly.

"Good thing it's non-alcoholic."

She makes a face. "Non-alcoholic champagne?"

I pour her a glass. "Just try it."

She lifts her glass and sniffs the liquid before drinking a small sip. "Hmm. Not bad."

"Are you hungry?"

"Starving. I had a sandwich for lunch but it fell apart and well...."

She motions to the front of her dress and I know exactly what happened.

"Let me feed you."

Thirty minutes later, Nova falls back in her chair with a moan. "I'm so full. I ate too much. I don't think I can move. Maybe you will have to carry me back to your chalet after all."

Our chalet, I think but don't correct her. She was weary enough to go on a date with me. She'll freak out if she knows I don't intend for her to return to her house ever again.

"It's too bad you can't move." I motion to the pool. "I had plans for us."

She springs to her feet, whips off her dress, and rushes to the pool but screeches to a halt before she reaches the water. "Oops. I forgot I have shoes on."

I kneel in front of her. "I've got you."

She places her hands on my shoulders as I unwind the silk straps from her calves until she can toe off her shoe. I massage her foot before switching to the other foot to remove her remaining shoe.

"I think I want someone to remove my shoes from now on."

I glance up at her. "I'm at your service."

She laughs and her stomach jiggles. She squeaks before grabbing her stomach. "No making fun of how fat I am."

I was excited when I noticed her belly had popped a few days ago. But I didn't mention it since I don't know what the protocol is. I'm glad I didn't as she appears insecure.

I push to my feet and place my hands on her belly. "You're not fat. You're pregnant. You're growing our baby in there. I can't wait to meet him or her."

She places her hands over mine. "Me too."

"I hope Sprog is a girl."

Her smile lights up her face. "You do?"

"A little girl who has your eyes and your smile. She'll be beautiful the way her mother is."

She rolls her eyes. "I'm not beautiful. Chloe's the beautiful one."

"Disagree. You're beautiful."

Her cheeks flush. I need to call her beautiful more often if this is the way she looks when I do. I lean down to kiss her. I miss her taste.

Her eyes catch on my mouth and she bites her bottom lip. It's an invitation I can't refuse.

My mouth is nearly on hers when the door bangs open and the waitress walks in. "Oops. Sorry."

"You can pick this up in the morning," I growl at her.

She hurries outside but it's too late. The moment has passed.

"Last one in the pool's a rotten egg!" Nova shouts before doing a cannonball into the pool. Water splashes everywhere.

"What are you waiting for?" she asks when she surfaces. "Do you enjoy being a rotten egg?"

She swims closer and splashes me. "Is Mr. Big Shot Football Player afraid of the water?"

I whip off my belt and her eyes follow the motion. My cock twitches but I warn it to calm down. Nova's interested but she's also weary. I don't want to push too hard too soon. The next time I sink into her, I want her one-hundred percent behind our relationship. Not hesitant.

"I'll have you know I grew up on an island."

"You did? I didn't know Double Crown grew up on an island."

Double Crown? She knows how much I hate the nickname. I'll get her back for teasing me. I pull off my t-shirt before kicking off my shoes and letting my pants drop to the ground. Her eyes travel over my body.

"Do you want me to turn around?"

Her gaze lifts to my face at my question. "Turn around?"

"To give you a better view."

She swallows. But my girl doesn't give in. She never does. She's a survivor.

"You're stalling. You're afraid of the water."

She splashes me again and I leap into the pool. I land next to her.

"Who's afraid now?" I ask.

"I'm not afraid. I was in the water long before you, chicken pants."

"Chicken pants?"

She shrugs. "If the scrawny legs fit."

"My legs are scrawny?"

I swim to her and she retreats as she splashes.

"Stick legs is what I've heard people call them." She giggles at her own joke.

And I'm done. I lunge for her and catch her before she has the chance to get away. She giggles as she splashes more water at me. I tighten my arms around her and do what I've wanted to do since the second she walked into the living room wearing those sexy sandals.

I meld my lips to hers. I can feel the smile on her soft lips and I smile in return before plunging my tongue into her mouth.

Her fingers dig into my shoulders as she moans. Her smell of wildflowers surround me and her taste fills my senses. It's a taste unique to Nova. A taste I'd recognize anywhere. A taste I hope to indulge in every day for the rest of my life.

I lift her higher until I can press my hard length into her core. She wraps her legs around me. I—

Ta dum.

Nova pulls away from me and glances around. "What's going on? Why am I hearing Netflix?"

"It's a movie." I motion to the screen I had set up. "A cockblocking movie," I mutter.

She bursts into laughter. Still laughing, she pushes away from me. I let her go since the moment has passed. Again.

She swims to her raft and gets on. "Movie time!"

I swim toward my own raft. I'd follow Nova anywhere. Even if it leads to blue balls.

Chapter 24

Love – scarier than a non-alcoholic fruity beer

NOVA

"Wait there," Hudson orders after he stops his truck in front of the side door to *Five Fathoms Brewing*.

I don't know what it says about me. But Hudson ordering me to wait in his growly voice has my entire body shivering in anticipation. I'll wait here. No problem at all.

He opens the passenger door and lifts me out of the truck. My body slides against his as he lowers me to the ground. I can feel each and every one of his hard muscles. My panties dampen, and I shiver.

His eyes flare. "Something you need, Sunshine?"

Him. I need him.

I wanted him last night after our date. But instead of removing my clothes and touching every inch of my body, he settled me in bed, kissed my forehead, wrapped his arm around my waist, and told me to go to sleep.

I could literally feel his hard length pushing into my back but when I squirmed against him for some much needed relief, he growled at me to sleep.

"You know what I need." I stick out my bottom lip and pout.

Hudson presses his lips against mine in a brief kiss. "Be good."

I waggle my eyebrows. "What if I want to be bad?"

He groans and his eyes fall closed before he places his forehead against mine. "Don't make this any more difficult than it is."

"Why is it difficult? It's not as if we haven't had sex before. I'm literally carrying proof we have."

"I want us to take things slow. Get to know each other better before we fall back into bed. Our relationship is not about sex. It's about us. Being together for the long haul."

I blow out a breath. I want to argue with him but how can I? He wants to be together with me for the long haul. The words cause panic to rear up but I push it down. I'm not freaking out in the parking lot of my business.

"I have another date planned for us tonight."

"What are we doing?"

"You'll find out tonight."

"You're cruel. You know I can't handle surprises."

He smirks. "I know."

I bat my eyelashes at him. "Don't you want to tell me?"

He chuckles. "Nope."

"I still win since you laughed."

"My nutty sunshine."

My heart warms every time he uses his nickname for me – Sunshine. I love how he thinks of me as his sunshine. But I'm not going to tell him as much. I'm not ready for the intimacy such a confession will bring.

"Sunshine can't be nutty."

He kisses my nose. "My sunshine can and is nutty."

I smile up at him.

"There she is," he mutters before melding his lips to mine.

I clutch his shoulders as he devours my mouth. Hudson doesn't play around when he kisses. He goes straight from sweet to panty-melting hot. When he growls and rips his mouth from mine, I mewl.

"Why are you stopping?"

"I want to strip you naked."

"Yes," I breathe out.

"We're in a parking lot, you need to get to work, and I just explained why I want to wait to have sex."

The long haul. Right. I nearly forgot.

And I'm a big fat liar. I didn't forget. I'm shoving those scary thoughts away. All scary thoughts shall henceforth be put in a jar marked 'do not open' and promptly forgotten.

He kisses my nose. "I'll pick you up at six."

"And then we'll go…"

He chuckles. "Nice try. It's a surprise."

He herds me toward the door. When I reach it, I turn around to wave. He's standing in front of his truck waiting for me to get inside. As if anything would happen to me in the parking lot of my brewery. Silly, overprotective man who's way too sexy for my own good.

I enter the brewery humming a song.

"Good. You're finished kissing Hudson. We can get started," Paisley says from where she's standing behind the bar.

Sophia, Chloe, and Maya are sitting on barstools in front of her. I join them.

"Ugh. I can't believe you're making me haul myself onto a barstool when I'm pregnant."

Maya hurries to help me. "Once you're seated, you'll be fine."

Sophia shakes her head. "I never expected you to be the first one of us to get pregnant."

"Who did you think it would be?"

She points to Maya. "Ms. Romantic."

Maya's cheeks darken and I frown. "Leave Maya alone."

Sophia shrugs. "What? She's been in love with Caleb forever. I figured they'd have a gazillion babies by now."

"We're friends," Maya mumbles.

"I'm friends with Lucas. But I also enjoy getting all sweaty and naked with him. If you get what I mean." Chloe waggles her eyebrows.

"Ahem." Paisley clears her throat. "We have business to attend to."

"We do?" My brow wrinkles. "And why are you standing behind the bar? Chloe never lets any of us stand behind the bar. I don't remember any meeting planned let alone one with you behind the bar."

Maya giggles. "Because you have love on the brain."

"The term is sex on the brain," Chloe corrects.

"Nope." Maya motions to my face. "This is the look of a woman in love."

I'm not in love. I agree I'm falling for Hudson but I'm not there yet. Love is scary and I'm not ready to face the fear.

Sophia leans close to study my face. I swat her away.

"I concur. She's in love."

"Another one bites the dust," Chloe sings.

Maya sighs. "This is the best. My friends are all falling in love."

"I'm not in love," I argue.

"You're not in love? Really?" She rolls her eyes. "You're having his baby."

"It was a mistake. I didn't realize my IUD needed to be replaced."

"You're living with him."

"Because he insisted. He wants to keep me and Sprog safe."

"You went on a date with him last night."

I gasp. "You weren't supposed to tell."

She snorts. "And you're not supposed to keep important secrets from us like how Hudson wants to have a relationship with you and built you a nursery."

"He built you a nursery?" Paisley asks.

"He built the baby a nursery."

"In his house," Maya says. "Where he wants you to live with him because you love him."

I scowl at her. I don't love Hudson. Do I think the man is sexy? Of course, I do. Every woman and quite a few men agree with me. It's why he was voted sexiest man in the NFL.

Do I think he's sweet? How can I not? He wants to take care of me. He cooks for me. He makes sure I don't have to clean.

Does my heart pound whenever he's near? To an alarming degree.

Holy smugglers. I love Hudson. How did this happen? I'm supposed to be protecting my heart from him. I won't survive if he leaves me. It'll be worse than when Mom died and I barely survived her death.

"Here." Paisley sets a beer down on the bar in front of me. "You look as if you could use this."

"I'm pregnant. I can't drink alcohol."

"This is a new non-alcoholic beer. It's a New England IPA. Since a NEIPA has a fruitier profile, it lends itself to a non-alcoholic variant more than a regular IPA."

"And now you know why I allowed Paisley behind my bar," Chloe mutters.

Sophia elbows her. "It's not your bar. It's our bar."

"I don't go on our Instagram account and post stuff, do I? Because you'd go mermaid on my ass."

"I wouldn't go mermaid on your ass."

"Really?" Chloe raises her eyebrows. "You didn't threaten to steal my phone when I posted a picture before?"

"You posted an image of you trying to pole dance while you were drunk. Drunken shenanigans is not the esthetic I'm going for."

"Your images are boring."

"Because no one's falling down drunk?"

"Yes!" Chloe cheers. "Exactly."

"Poor Lucas," Sophia says. "I don't know how he deals with you."

Chloe grins. "He loves me."

"Speaking of love." Maya points to me. "Someone is freaking out because she just realized she loves Hudson."

Crap on a rumrunner. I thought they'd forgotten all about me. I should be so lucky.

"This beer is good," I tell Paisley.

She pushes her glasses up her nose. "You haven't even tasted it yet."

I try a sip. "Yum. It's fruity but not too fruity. It still tastes of beer."

"It's cute you think you can change the subject," Maya says.

I purse my lips. "The subject is the beer. We're here to taste test Paisley's latest creations."

"No. We're here to make sure you aren't freaking out after you realized you love Hudson."

"I'm not freaking out."

"You aren't? You're not already packing your suitcases in your head?"

"As long as I'm carrying his baby, Hudson will follow me wherever I go."

Maya sighs. "I never thought the big, bad football hero would be romantic."

I wish I was her. Excited for romance. But I'm not. I'm too worried about what my loving Hudson means for him.

I'm going to lose him. I lose everyone I love.

I'm sorry, Hudson.

Chapter 25

Bribery – is A-OK with Nova as long as she gets what she wants

NOVA

"You ready?" Hudson asks when I step outside of the brewery into the parking lot.

I beam up at him. I am ready. I've thought about it all day and I'm just going to enjoy Hudson for now. I'm not making any big decisions until baby Sprog is born. I have nearly four months to enjoy Hudson and being pregnant.

After then.... Well, after then, I'll figure it out.

"We don't have to go out."

I frown at him. "What? You promised me a date."

"If you're not in the mood or aren't feeling well, we can go home. I'll cook you some of my famous chicken noodle soup and we'll watch a movie."

I raise my eyebrows. "Your chicken noodle soup is famous now?"

"You moaned the entire time you ate it."

I roll my eyes. "Because I was hungry."

He shakes his head. "What'll it be? Home or date? No pressure."

"It's hard to decide when I don't know what the date is."

"I'm not telling you the surprise."

I blow out a breath. "You're mean."

"You're impatient."

I place a hand on my baby bump. "I can be patient."

He lays his hand over mine. "I can't wait to meet Sprog."

I love how excited he is to meet our baby. He didn't even want a baby to begin with. Hold on. I don't know if he didn't want a baby.

"Did you want children before you met me?"

He opens the truck passenger door and lifts me into my seat. He reaches across me to buckle the seatbelt but I grab his hand to stop him.

"Are you going to answer me?"

"In the truck," he grumbles.

Uh oh. Mr. Grouchypants is back from his vacation.

"And?" I ask once he's sitting beside me. "Did you want children before you knocked me up?"

He places a hand on my thigh and squeezes. "I never thought about having children before."

"You're thirty-two. You must have thought about it."

He switches on the engine and backs out of the parking space before speaking again. "My entire focus has been on my football career."

"But your football career ended three years ago." He cringes. "I'm sorry. I know it's a sore subject."

"It's not a sore subject."

"Which is why you cringe or shut down every time I mention the end of your football career."

"When I returned to Smuggler's Hideaway, I was too busy building the resort to worry about anything else."

"Don't think I didn't notice how you changed the subject."

"I thought the subject was whether I wanted children before you."

I wag a finger at him. "I'll allow you to avoid the sore subject for now."

"Good." He pulls into a parking spot in front of *Smuggler's Cove*. "Because we're here."

I stare at the restaurant. "We can't be here."

"Why not?"

"The *Smuggler Reenactment Dinner* is tonight. It's impossible to get tickets."

"I got tickets."

"Did you bribe someone?" He shrugs and I gasp. "You did! You bribed someone." I giggle. "You're getting the hang of Smuggler's Hideaway after all."

He kisses my nose. "I did grow up here."

"What are you waiting for? Let's go. Let's go." I reach for the door handle and he growls.

"Wait for me."

"Hurry up, Grumpystilskin. There are smugglers waiting."

"Smugglers wait for no one," he claims but he does get out of the truck and walk around to open my door.

I jump into his arms. "Let's go, Mr. Grumpalotoulos."

"Am I Greek now?"

"Tall, dark, and handsome is Greek."

He smirks. "You think I'm handsome."

"Duh. I made this baby with you, didn't I?"

He sets me on my feet and places his hand on my lower back to guide me into the restaurant. It's crowded when we enter. I start to push my way through the throng of people but Hudson maneuvers so he's in front of me and can lead the way.

"Reservation for Hudson," he barks at the waitress.

I wave to her. "Hi, Hazel!"

"Nova, how are you doing?" She opens her arms to hug me but Hudson growls at her.

"Sorry, the caveman is out tonight."

She giggles. "I heard you snagged the most eligible bachelor on Smuggler's Hideaway." She nods to my belly. "Congratulations."

"Thanks." I thread my arm through Hudson's.

She grins. "The girl banned from cheerleading is now dating the football player."

I roll my eyes. "I wasn't banned from cheerleading. You can't ban someone from cheerleading for life."

She snorts. "I was there. Broken bones happened. They totally banned you for life."

"It wasn't my fault."

"Hey!" someone behind her shouts. "Can we get some service here?"

Hazel rolls her eyes. "Sorry. The *Smuggler Reenactment Dinner* always brings out the tourists."

Which is the entire idea. Once the summer ends, the number of tourists visiting the island dwindles. The idea of the *Smuggler Reenactment Dinner* is to bring in tourists during the offseason. Based on how crowded the restaurant is, it's working.

"Come on." She grabs two menus. "I'll show you to your table."

We follow her to a private table in the corner. From here, we can watch the action but it's not as loud.

"Best table in the house." Hazel slaps the menus on the table. "You're a lucky girl. It's a set menu tonight but you can order off the menu if you want."

"How much did you bribe the owner?" I ask Hudson.

He shrugs.

I was joking. He's clearly not. "You did bribe the owner."

"You and your friends were planning a heist to steal all the tickets to tonight's event. I had no choice."

Hazel nods. "Good decision. You know they would have totally pulled off a heist."

I scowl. "The tickets are electronic. A heist wouldn't have helped."

"Except the mayor's office has ten paper tickets."

I lift my menu to hide behind it since I'm a sucky liar. "I didn't know."

Hazel giggles as she walks off. "Good luck with her."

"He's lucky to have me," I holler after her.

Hudson grunts.

"I interpret your grunt as agreement." I lay my menu on the table. "When does the action start?"

"You're not mad I bribed the owner?"

I wave my hand in dismissal. "Of course not. I got what I wanted."

"You're easy."

"Duh." I point to my belly.

He reaches across the table for my hand. "I didn't mean you're easy in that way."

"I know, but it's sweet you're worried."

"I'm not sweet," he grumbles.

The door flies open and a gang of bootleggers rush into the restaurant. "Shush. The reenactment is starting."

"We need to hide. Where can we hide?" The first bootlegger asks as he scans the restaurant.

I raise my hand. "Over here! Over here!"

The group starts toward us but Hudson growls at them and they halt.

I slap Hudson's shoulder. "Don't ruin my fun."

"You're not hiding a group of five men under our table."

"Spoilsport."

The smugglers decide to hide under another table. They've barely had a chance to conceal themselves before the door bangs open again and a group of policemen enter.

"It's Weston." I wave at Sophia's brother. "Hey, Weston!"

He saunters toward me. "Have you seen any smugglers this evening?"

I widen my eyes and feign surprise. "Smugglers? Here in the *Smuggler's Cove* restaurant in the town of *Smuggler's Rest* on the island of *Smuggler's Hideaway*. Why would there be smugglers here?"

"You're obviously hiding them."

I waggle my eyebrows at him. "Do you want to look under my table?"

"No one's looking under our table," Hudson grumbles.

"This is cause for suspicion. Lift up the tablecloth or I'm hauling you into the police station."

"You can try," Hudson growls.

I clasp my chest. "Oh no, Hudson. This will be your third offense. You'll never get out of prison in time for the birth of the baby."

I bat my eyelashes at Weston. "Can you let him go this one time?" I place a hand on my belly. "I'm pregnant."

Weston scowls at Hudson. "You knocked up an innocent woman. And you haven't married her to salvage her reputation. You are a criminal."

I jump to my feet. "Just look under our table. I promise we didn't do anything wrong."

Hudson stands and moves behind me. "Don't touch Nova, or we'll have problems."

"What kind of problems?" Weston asks.

I flip the tablecloth up to reveal the empty space. "See? No smugglers here. In fact, we haven't seen any smugglers at all. The town and island are not living up to their reputation. I'm mighty disappointed."

Weston glares at Hudson. "I'll let you off this time but if you step out of line again, I can guarantee you won't be free when your baby is born."

I clutch Hudson's hand. "He won't step out of line. I'll make sure of it."

Weston tips his hat to me. "He's lucky to have you."

He saunters away to continue the search for the smugglers and we settle back into our chairs to watch.

"This is too much fun."

"I need to start a bank account for all the bribes and bail money I'm going to need with you around."

"I promise to behave." I wink.

"I don't."

My panties dampen at the growl of the promise of those words.

"I'm going to hold you to those words."

My worry about the future is completely forgotten as his eyes flare.

I'll worry about the future tomorrow.

Or maybe next week.

Or maybe after the baby is born.

For now, I'm throwing my arms in the air and enjoying the ride.

Chapter 26

Touchdown – when Hudson finally makes it to the endzone

HUDSON

"Did you have fun?" I ask Nova as we enter our chalet.

"It was the best. Thank you for getting tickets. I loved how involved the audience was."

I chuckle. "I don't think anyone expected you to throw bread at the police."

She shrugs. "Weston deserved it."

I frown. "What did he do?"

"What didn't he do? When we were in high school, he was always torturing Sophia and the rest of us somehow."

I relax. She's not referring to the present day.

I pull her into my arms. "I'm glad you had a good time."

She smiles up at me and my entire body warms. Her smile can warm the darkest corners of my soul. I should probably let her go. She deserves someone who's as happy as she is, but I'm not going to. She's the only person who can make me happy. Her and the baby.

"Did you have fun?" she asks.

"I was with you."

She rolls her eyes. "That's not an answer, caveman."

I tuck her hair behind her ear. "Yes, it is." I kiss her forehead. "Being with you is the only thing that matters."

"Does this mean you're removing the no sex rule?"

"There wasn't a no sex rule."

"Sure felt like there was a no sex rule when you tucked me into bed like a five-year-old last night."

"I don't want you to think this relationship is only about the sex."

"I don't. But I do think I'm sexually frustrated."

"Sexually frustrated?"

"Pregnancy increases a woman's libido." She pouts. "You're not going to deny me again, are you? I thought you wanted to take care of me."

I growl. "I do want to take care of you."

"There's more ways to take care of me than making me chicken noodle soup."

She bats her eyelashes at me and I'm lost. How can I deny the woman I'm falling in love with?

"If we have sex—"

"Yes!"

I place a finger over her lips. "I said if."

She nips at my finger until I move it. "You'll give in."

"Fine. When we have sex, you have to promise to tell me if anything hurts."

"Grumpy dude, you don't have to worry about the baby. You won't harm Sprog."

"I know. But sex can be uncomfortable during pregnancy."

She giggles. "I should probably be turned off by how clinical you sound but it's sexy how you read all those pregnancy books. Lead me to your lair, grumpy man of mine. Show me what I've been missing."

I'll show her what she's been missing all right. I pick her up and carry her in my arms to the bedroom. I lay her down on the bed and she sighs.

"I love your bedroom. It fits you."

I kneel between her legs. "It's *our* bedroom from now on."

"You're moving awful fast for someone who hated me for the past three years."

I squeeze her hips. "I never hated you. I wanted you but was denying myself."

She rubs a hand over her belly. "But the denying yourself had a spectacular finish."

"I'll move your stuff in here tomorrow."

She holds up her hands. "Hey, now. I never agreed to move bedrooms."

"Didn't disagree either." She can fight me on this, but she'll lose. I don't want her staying in the guest room down the hall. I want her in here in this bed with me.

"If you don't want to stay with me every night, you can stay in the guest bedroom. But there won't be any sex."

"You're denying me sex unless I give in?"

"No, I'm explaining how I don't think we should have sex until you're ready to move into this bedroom with me."

She scowls at me. "I think I enjoyed it better when you grunted instead of spoke."

"You're annoyed because I'm right."

She stares at me for a moment and I hold my breath. I want her in my bedroom with me, but I don't want to push her too hard. I don't want to scare her off.

"Fine," she mutters. "I'll move in here but I'm adding pillows and throw blankets and color."

"I don't give a fuck what you do as long as you're in this bed with me every night from now on."

"For someone who barely talks, you sure know the right thing to say."

"Talking is done. Time to move on."

I stand at the end of the bed and remove her boots. Once they're out of the way, I lean forward to pull her leggings down her legs leaving her in a fuzzy, white sweater.

"Arms up." She hesitates and I repeat the order. "Arms up."

"Promise you won't make fun of how fat I am."

I growl. "You are not fat."

She lifts her arms slowly and I don't waste any time bunching her sweater together and removing it.

She's a vision on my bed with her long brown hair spread out over my pillow and her body covered only in her pink panties and bra. Her breasts are practically spilling out of her bra. Her stomach where our baby is growing is obviously noticeable. I place my hand on it.

"You're beautiful."

"I'm not b—"

"No. You are beautiful to me. I hope our daughter looks like you."

"What if Sprog's a boy?"

"I'll love the baby no matter what."

Her smile is wistful. "Me, too."

As much as I enjoy watching her become wistful over our child, my cock reminds me I have other matters to attend to. I toy with the waistband of her panties. She shivers in response and spreads her legs.

"Something you want?"

"Yep." She nods.

"Which is?"

"You know what I want."

"My mouth?"

She bites her bottom lip. "Yes, please."

"Your wish is my command."

I've been dying to taste her again since the first night we spent together. Is her taste as sweet as I remember? Will she make those little moans and sighs the way she did last time? Will she scream when she comes apart?

Time to find out.

I draw her panties down her legs and throw them on the floor. I guide my hands up her legs and watch goosebumps form in my wake. She can't hide her reaction to me.

"Widen your legs."

She doesn't hesitate. I fucking love how eager she is.

I grasp her ankles and pull her to the edge of the bed before kneeling in front of her. I glide my nose along her lips and inhale. The scent of wildflowers fills my senses. I will never look at wildflowers the same again.

Her hands clutch my hair and she pushes her core toward my face. I chuckle at my impatient woman.

I spread her lips with my fingers and find her clit with my tongue. I rub circles around it until her fingernails dig into my head. Only then do I suck her clit into my mouth.

"Yes," she hisses. "More."

If she wants more, she gets more. Whatever my sunshine wants, I will move the earth to get for her. All she has to do is ask. Or beg.

I circle her pussy with my finger.

"Yes."

I reward her by inching my finger inside her. I groan at how hot and wet she is. She's dripping for me and I've barely touched her.

I pump one finger in and out of her while I play with her clit with my mouth.

"Yes. Yes. Yes," she chants.

I add a second finger and increase my pace while I suck on her clit.

"Yes!" she shouts as her walls clamp down on my fingers with her release.

I continue to pump into her until she collapses on the bed. I kiss her thigh before standing.

"Next time you come, you scream my name."

Her face is flushed and her eyes are sparkling. "First you have to make me scream."

"Don't you worry. I'll make you scream."

I quickly remove my clothes before climbing into bed with her. "On your side." She rolls to her side to face me. "I want to watch when you climax."

Her eyes flare. "Me, too."

I lift her leg and place it over mine, opening her up to me. "Are you ready for me, Sunshine?" She nods and I hitch my cock at her entrance.

I watch those exotic eyes I'm obsessed with as I slide home.

Home. This is home. This is where I'm meant to be. Where I'm meant to spend my life.

With Nova.

Chapter 27

Slow down – not going to happen if Hudson has anything to say about it

NOVA

I wake to Hudson's arm banded around me and his giant hand on my belly. This is everything I ever wanted. A man I love, a baby I love. A family.

I cuddle into Hudson's warmth. I have a family who I love. Love.

My chest tightens and breathing becomes impossible as panic seizes me. Love. I can't love Hudson and the baby. Everyone I love dies.

I should leave. I should run away.

I lift Hudson's arm and start to scoot away.

"Where are you going?" He growls and I startle.

I think of a lie as fast as I can. "Bathroom. Baby Sprog makes me have to pee."

He pats my ass. "Hurry back. I have plans for you this morning."

I shiver at the promise in his voice. Hudson is very good – exceptional actually – at keeping his promises.

"Okay," I squeak and rush toward the door.

He sits up. "Where are you going?"

"Bathroom." And now I've said the word twice, I really do need to go. I dance from foot to foot.

He points to his attached bathroom. "The bathroom is right here."

Mermaids on fire! How could I forget about the whole moving into his room thing? Probably because I was panicking about loving him. About getting everything I've ever dreamed of. About what happens to all the people I love.

My heart races in my chest and my breathing increases until I'm fighting for air. I can't answer Hudson. I can't speak.

I rush out of the room to the guest bedroom and bathroom. I slam the door to the bathroom behind me and lock it before sinking to the floor.

I'm okay. I'm okay. I'm okay. I'm okay.

I repeat the words over and over until my heart slows and I can finally breathe. I wipe the sweat from my forehead before standing. I grip the edge of the vanity and switch on the water. I splash cold water on my face.

What am I going to do?

Obviously, I can't move into Hudson's bedroom. Maybe I should move back home. Maybe I should end this relationship with Hudson before it gets serious.

I place my hand on my baby belly. Before it gets any more serious, I should say.

Before anyone gets hurt.

Mind made up, I jump in the shower for a quick wash. I don't bother drying my hair, though. I need to pack and move home. I can't wait. If I wait, I'll fall deeper in love with Hudson.

I hurry into my bedroom. Where is my suitcase? Is it in the walk-in closet? Or—

"Why didn't you come back to bed?"

"AH!" I scream at Hudson's question. I clutch my chest. "What are you doing in here?"

He stands from the chair and prowls toward me. "Wrong question."

My brow wrinkles. "Wrong question? How can a question I want an answer to be wrong?"

He stops in front of me and crosses his arms over his chest. Since he's not wearing a shirt, I get to watch as his muscles bunch with the movement. I nearly lift my hand to touch him before I remember.

I need to leave.

"We agreed you'd move into my bedroom last night. But now you're showering in the guest bathroom."

"All my stuff is in there."

"Why are you running scared?"

"I'm not scared."

He palms my neck and squeezes. "It's okay to be scared. Moving in together is a big deal."

It's the opening I need. "I think we should slow down. Get to know each other better before we take the next step."

He cocks an eyebrow. "Get to know each other better? We've known each other our entire lives."

I'll play his game. "You think you know everything about me?"

"Not everything but I know the important stuff. I know you're the best salesperson, *Five Fathoms Brewing* could ever want. I know you love to swim but hate the feel of sand between your toes and salt drying on your skin from the ocean. I know you're loyal to your friends. I know your smile lights up the room. I know you still grieve for the loss of your parents – your mom especially – but you don't let the grief overwhelm you. I know you're going to be the best mom our child could ever want."

My chest warms. He does know me. It's almost as if he loves me the way I love him.

"What I don't know is why you're panicking and running away from me when you should be running to me whenever you feel panicked."

The warmth disappears as ice fills my veins at his words.

"I'm not panicking," I deny. I am not discussing this with him. This is my secret I'll take to my grave with me.

He places a hand on my cheek. "You are panicking, Sunshine."

I open my mouth to deny it again but he places a finger over my mouth to silence me.

"No, Sunshine. You aren't denying what is obvious to see. You think I don't know what someone having a panic attack looks like?"

"How—"

"No. We're not discussing my experience with panic attacks. You're not putting me off any longer. Why are you panicking?"

"Maybe it's none of your business."

"It sure as hell is my business when you're planning to run away from me."

"I'm not running away."

He scowls. "You were muttering to yourself about your suitcase when you came dashing out of the bathroom."

"Maybe I need my suitcase to move my stuff into your bedroom."

He lifts an eyebrow. "I never pegged Nova Myers for a coward."

I glare at him. "I'm not a coward! How dare you say I am!"

"If the shoe fits…" He shrugs.

My nostrils flare. How dare he? I am the furthest thing from a coward. He's not a grump. He's an asshole.

"I am not a coward. A coward doesn't hold her mother's hand as she dies. A coward doesn't go to school the next day despite knowing everyone pities her. A coward doesn't get up every single day and smile at life despite how life has kicked her down time and time again."

My chest heaves as I fight to keep myself from hyperventilating.

"If you're not a coward, why are you running away from me? From the life we can have together?"

"Because I don't want you to die!" I scream as tears burst from my eyes and course down my cheeks.

Hudson wipes the tears from my face. "I'm not going to die."

"Yes, you are! Everyone I love dies."

He wraps his arms around me and hauls me to him. I cling to him. I shouldn't. I should push him away. Now that he knows the truth, he won't care if I leave.

"I'm sorry about your mom and dad. I can't imagine how devastating it was to lose them at such a young age."

"It was horrible," I blubber. "I miss them so much."

He guides his hand up and down my back as he sways me from side to side. "I know you do, Sunshine. I know you do."

"Our baby won't have my mom as her grandmother or my dad as her grandfather. They're missing everything."

"We'll tell them about baby Sprog. And we'll tell the baby about your parents. We'll make sure Sprog knows how wonderful they were."

We? He doesn't get it. There can't be a we. I push away from him.

"We aren't going to do anything because I'm leaving."

"You are not leaving," he grumbles.

"You can't keep me here!"

"I'm not keeping you here. You want to be here."

"It doesn't matter what I want. I can't be here. Don't you get it? Everyone I love dies. I'm saving you."

"Not everyone you love dies."

"Really?" I start counting off on my fingers. "One. My dad died before I was ten. Two. My mom died when I was in high school."

I wave my fingers at him and he catches my hand.

"One. Sophia is still alive. Two. So is Chloe. Three. As is Maya. Four. And Paisley."

"They don't count."

He raises an eyebrow. "Should I tell your friends you don't love them? You don't consider them family?"

"It's not the same thing."

"What about Jack and Lily? Did they not step in to become your pseudo parents when your mom died? Did they not invite you to every family gathering? Did they not make you feel like family? Should I let Lily know you don't consider her family?"

"I do but…"

He palms my cheeks. "Not everyone you love dies."

"But…"

"I don't blame you for having this fear. I'd be a complete basket case if I was orphaned in high school."

"I'm not a basket case."

"No, you're sunshine and happiness and the light of my life."

"The light of your life?"

His lips tip up and I can't resist lifting my hand to touch his lips. "Why do you think I resisted you for so long?"

My brow wrinkles. "Because I'm the light of your life? I'm confused."

He chuckles. "No, because I didn't want to dim your light. I'm a complete grump who ruins everything he touches."

"I'm even more confused now. Ruin everything you touch? What have you ruined thus far? Did you forget you have two Super Bowl Championship rings? Or maybe you forgot you have a successful resort so popular guests need to reserve a year in advance? Or what about the mounds of money in your bank account?" I snort. "Ruin everything you touch, my smuggler bottom."

"If I agree I don't ruin everything I touch, you have to agree not everyone you love dies." He holds out a hand. "Do we have a deal?"

I start to reach for his hand. "I'll agree you made some valid points I will think about more later."

"And you'll move into my bedroom and live in this chalet with me as a couple."

I narrow my eyes at him. "You can't change the deal after offering your hand."

"You know you want to stay with me."

I roll my eyes. "I do, do I?"

"Yep. Because I'll give you multiple orgasms every night, make you soup whenever you want, hold your hair back when you get sick, drive you wherever you need to go, open every door for you, and be your champion when you're feeling down."

"You're supposed to be a grump. Not a romantic man."

He grunts. "Not romantic."

He has no idea. He's romantic and oh so very tempting.

"You're not scared, are you?"

My nostrils flare. Scared? I'll show him. I slap my hand into his. "Fine. Deal. But if you die, it's your fault, not mine."

"I'm not going to die." He kisses my forehead. "Promise."

"Don't make promises you can't keep."

"I don't, Sunshine. I don't."

I blow out a breath. I hope he's right. I hope my bad luck doesn't extend to him. Because if he leaves me, I don't think I'll survive.

Chapter 28

Special teams – Hudson's brothers who are one step up from heathens

HUDSON

"Hurry up, Nova. We're going to be late."

She peeks her head out of the bathroom. "It's not my fault. If you wouldn't have come home from your workout all sweaty and sexy, I wouldn't have jumped you."

I chuckle. "You came before I managed to get your clothes off."

She glares at me. "Did not." She shuts the door in my face.

I message my mom to let her know we're going to be late. I barely have a chance to put my phone in my pocket before it rings in response.

"You can't be late," Mom hisses.

"Nova isn't ready yet."

"But what if her family shows up before you?"

"You'll be fine. Her family is nice."

"Jack and Lily are millionaires."

I chuckle. "You would be, too, if you'd let me give you some of my money."

"It's bad enough you bought a house for us."

I sigh. I'm not having this argument again. "We'll be there as soon as we can."

"Thank you."

I hang up the phone and knock on the bathroom door. "Mom's freaking out. Can you—"

The door opens and I lose the ability to speak. Nova is dressed in a sweater dress that clings to all of her curves. Those breasts I love to suck on and those hips I love to hold onto while I sink into her from behind are on display.

My cock twitches. I clear my throat and think of the total offensive yards I ran my final year in the NFL. Once I have my cock under control, I step forward and kiss her forehead.

"You look beautiful."

Her nose wrinkles. "It's not too tight?"

I place her hand over my semi-hard cock. "No."

She giggles as she squeezes.

I groan and shackle her wrist to pull her away. "We can't be late, my little temptress. Mom's freaking out about meeting your family."

She smiles up at me. "I love how you refer to my friends as my family."

"Because they are."

I'm going to show her she can love someone and they won't die. I never want to witness the terror in Nova's eyes ever again like when she told me everyone she loves dies and she's afraid I'm going to die, too.

She didn't admit it. But she loves me. And I will do everything in my power to show her I'm worthy of her love. She is the one good thing I won't ruin. Not this time.

I place my hand on her lower back and guide her out of the chalet to my truck. When I help her onto the passenger seat, I can't stop myself from digging my fingers into her hips. She shivers in response.

I kiss her quickly. "Behave."

Her eyes widen. "What did I do?"

"You're tempting me, Sunshine."

She smirks. "It's not on purpose."

"Liar." I tweak her nose before shutting her door and hurrying around to the driver's side.

"Why is your mom freaking out?" she asks as I drive toward the town of Smuggler's Rest.

"She thinks of Jack and Lily as Smuggler's Hideaway royalty."

"Sometimes I forget how much money they have. They don't act the way I expect millionaires to act."

"Not all millionaires are assholes," I grumble.

She pats my hand on the steering wheel. "There's no reason to go into grump mode. I know you're not an asshole millionaire. Honestly, sometimes I forget how much money you have. And then you close down the swimming pool for us to watch a movie while floating in the water and I remember."

I frown. "I wasn't trying to show off my wealth."

"I didn't say you were." She retracts her hand but I grab it. I like touching Nova. Her skin is soft and feels smooth compared to my rough hands.

"Who do you think will be the most trouble? My money's on Chloe."

I snort. "Did you forget about my brothers? Logan's okay as long as he's not working on some special project in chemistry. But Owen, Sawyer, and Brooks? Any one of them could win the crown for causing the most trouble."

"I like your brothers."

"You would. You were a troublemaker in high school, too."

"I was not. Sophia and Chloe were the troublemakers."

I raise an eyebrow. "And you didn't follow their lead?"

She shrugs. "They had good ideas."

"Good ideas? They stole the pirate mascot from Pirate's Perch and the raccoon mascot from Rogue's Landing and then let the animals loose on the football field."

She giggles. "We didn't think the parrot would repeat everything the coach said. You have to admit it was hilarious listening to a parrot fly over the field shouting *there's a raccoon loose on the field, there's a raccoon loose on the field, time out, time out.*"

It was hilarious. Especially since the opposing team freaked out when they saw the raccoon and ran off the field. We won by default when they refused to return after the raccoon and parrot were caught.

"We're here." I park on the street and scan the area. None of Nova's family is here yet. Good. Mom won't kill me for being late.

The front door flies open while we're walking up the sidewalk. "Oh." Brooks frowns. "It's you."

Nova places a hand on her belly and smiles at him. "Nice to know my baby's uncle is excited to meet her."

His eyes light up. "Her? Are you having a girl?"

I grunt. "We don't know."

"The baby mooned us during our scan so we couldn't see if Sprog is a he or a she," she explains.

"The baby mooned you?" Brooks asks. "I blame the Clark genes."

"So do I," Nova whispers.

Three vehicles arrive and park behind my truck.

"They're here!" Brooks shouts into the house.

"They're here. They're here," Mom mutters as she rushes to the door.

Nova flashes her a smile. "Don't worry. My family will love you the way I do."

Mom sniffs before throwing her arms around Nova. "I love you, too."

"What's going on? Why is everyone crying and hugging on the porch?" Sophia asks as she arrives with her boyfriend, Flynn, and Nova's friends, Maya and Paisley.

Jack and Lily, with their son Weston, are right behind them. Chloe, Lucas, and their daughter bring up the rear.

"Is everything okay?" Lily asks. "How can I help? I have whiskey, chocolate cake, and a husband who's not afraid to knock sense into a son."

Jack grunts. "I never knocked sense into Weston."

Weston smirks. "Because I've got sense all on my own."

"Not likely," Sophia mutters.

Mom untangles herself from Nova and I claim my sunshine. "You, okay?" I whisper to her and she nods. "No more tears." I wipe the liquid from her cheeks.

"Gross," Brooks declares. "I'm going inside."

Mom clears her throat. "Why don't we all go inside?"

I herd everyone into the living room and close the door behind us.

"Shall I make the introductions?" Nova doesn't wait for a response before beginning. "These are my friends, Paisley, Maya, Chloe, and Sophia. The man hanging onto Sophia is her boyfriend, Flynn. The man with Chloe is her husband, Lucas. The girl with them is their daughter, Natalia. The man standing on his own is Weston. Sophia's brother and Flynn's best friend." She nods to Lily. "And this woman is Lily, my substitute mom, and Jack, my substitute dad."

"I prefer the term bonus mom," Lily says.

Nova immediately gives in. "Okay, bonus mom and bonus dad." She sweeps her arm to the other side of the room where my brothers and parents are.

"And on the other side of the room, we have the Clark family. Jacob and Emma are the proud parents of five boys. You know Hudson. The others are Brooks, Sawyer, Owen, and Logan."

"Your brothers are much younger than you," Chloe remarks.

Sawyer smirks. "Dad knocked up Mom in high school with Hudson. The rest of us came later."

Dad slaps him upside the head. "What? It's not a secret."

"We're trying to make a good impression on Nova's family."

Owen barks out a laugh. "Too late."

I lean down to whisper to Nova. "Told you my brothers would cause more trouble than Chloe."

"Hey!" Chloe shouts. "No fair. I'm not a troublemaker anymore."

Lucas barks out a laugh. "No, my wildcat is perfectly tame now. She didn't phone the police while I was on duty and claim her sheep were loose."

"There was a sheep loose."

"Because you let it loose."

Chloe shrugs. "How else was I going to get you to come home early?" She places her hands over her stepdaughter's ears. "I bought lingerie and Natalia had a meeting at school."

Natalia shoves Chloe's hands away. "Gross, Mom. I don't need to know about your s-e-x life."

Brooks raises his arm in the air. "I want to hear."

I slap his shoulder. "Behave."

"But it's more fun to not behave." He waggles his eyebrows.

Mom giggles. "And here I was worried about everyone getting along."

Lily marches to her and threads her arm through hers. "Let me help you get dinner ready. I can give you some tips on surviving the teenage years when your teenagers are sex-crazed."

"Hey!" Paisley shouts after them. "I wasn't sex-crazed."

"And I didn't walk in on you watching porn either," Lily says.

"Porn is perfectly normal."

"It was an orgy. I had to give you the talk about polyamorous relationships."

"I want the talk on polyamorous relationships," Brooks says.

"Me, too," Owen agrees.

"Definitely," Sawyer adds.

Logan sighs. "My brothers are all heathens."

"I didn't get the talk on polyamorous relationships," Sophia claims.

"Because you've been in love with your brother's best friend since puberty," her mom says.

Sophia frowns. "I have no comeback. It's true."

Flynn scowls. "You don't have to look sad about it."

They begin to bicker and I grasp Nova's wrist before dragging her down the hallway to my old bedroom.

"Are you happy?" I ask.

Her smile nearly blinds me. "This is the best day ever. Thank you for arranging this."

I kiss her nose. "I'll arrange anything you need or want."

"Gag!" Owen shouts through the door. "I thought you were having sex."

"Give us a minute!" Nova shouts back. "I have on boots and tights."

I glare at her and she bursts into laughter. "Your face."

I pull her into my arms and enjoy the feel of her body trembling against mine as she laughs. I'll be the butt of her joke every day for the rest of my life as long as I can feel her in my arms at the end of the day.

Chapter 29

Oops – when you accidentally tell your baby daddy the truth

NOVA

I frown at my phone. The date can't be right. I can't be nearly twenty-four weeks pregnant already. There must be a mistake.

I open my work calendar to check the date when I met Hudson at the *Hideaway Haven Resort* to convince him to give *Five Fathoms Brewing* a try. There it is – *convince the grump to buy our beer* is written in bold and underlined in my agenda. I write down the date before checking my pregnancy tracker app.

"Ugh!" I throw my phone on the table when I realize I didn't make a mistake. I am nearly twenty-four weeks pregnant.

"What's wrong?"

I grasp my chest and whirl around to face Hudson. "Where did you come from?"

"The same place I come from every morning."

He runs every morning. Too bad the weather has gotten colder. I miss watching sweat roll down his naked abs.

"But it's raining."

"An athlete doesn't stop training because it's raining."

But Hudson isn't an athlete anymore. He's a resort owner. Does he miss playing in the NFL? Does he wish he wasn't back home on Smuggler's Hideaway? Does he long for the glitz and glamor of being a star?

"What's wrong?" He repeats his question before I have the chance to quiz him.

"I didn't say anything is wrong."

"You threw your phone on the table."

"It's my prerogative to throw my phone wherever I want."

"Fine." He stalks toward me, grabs my hand, and pulls me out of the chair. "I'll sex it out of you."

"Sex it out of me? Is this a proper term?"

"Don't give a shit what it's called."

He lifts me in his arms and carries me to the bedroom. "Do you want to shower with me or shall I just eat you out now before I shower?"

Despite knowing he's using sex to get information from me, my body tingles in response to his question. I love it when Hudson puts his mouth on me. The man sure knows how to use his mouth. But a shower with him is also good. I love touching his muscles when they're hot and wet from water pouring down on us.

"Um…" I bite my lip. "Can I have both?"

"I'm not going down on you in the shower again. I nearly drowned last time."

"It's not my fault."

He lifts an eyebrow. "It's not your fault you shoved my face into the drain?"

"I didn't shove your face into the drain." My cheeks heat. It's possible I got carried away. It's his fault. He got me worked up and I needed release before I burst.

He sighs. "I guess I'm drowning in the shower. Or you could tell me what's wrong."

I giggle. "You think I'll tell you what's wrong rather than have sex with you? Have you met me?"

He sets me on my feet. My nipples harden as my breasts rub against the front of his shirt. My panties dampen as I imagine him sucking on my breasts. I love it when he lavishes my chest with attention.

"My sunshine is a sex fiend."

"I'm not a sex fiend. I'm pregnant."

Or, at least, I hope I'm still pregnant. What if there's something wrong with the baby? Maybe I should call my doctor again. Dr. Katz is getting used to me. She didn't even bother to yell at me the last time I phoned her after hours.

Hudson sits on the end of the bed and draws me near until I'm standing between his spread legs. He places his hands on my cheeks.

"What's wrong, Sunshine? You look devastated."

I nibble on my lip as I consider my answer.

"You're going to think I'm a hypochondriac."

"No, I won't."

"You promise?"

"Nova, my sunshine, you're allowed to worry about your health. It's natural you worry more than normal. Both of your parents died of cancer at young ages. Of course, you worry."

"You don't think I'm a worry wart?"

"You're too beautiful to be a wart."

I slap his shoulder. "You know what I mean."

He catches my hand and kisses my palm. "I know what you mean and I don't give a shit. Worry as much as you want. Just don't worry about worrying."

"You make it sound easy."

"Nothing's easy in this life."

I don't know. Loving Hudson is pretty easy. I nearly open my mouth to say as much but manage to clamp my lips shut before I admit I love him. He has enough to deal with without me blurting out how much I love him.

"Come on, Sunshine. Tell me why you're worried. If I don't know why you're worried, I can't handle it."

"Handle it?" I scowl at him. "You don't handle me."

He snorts. "No one can handle you. I meant we can contact the doctor or get you medicine or consult a pregnancy book. Whatever it is, we'll figure it out and handle it."

"You always know the right thing to say."

He grunts.

"Except when you grunt."

His fingers dig into my hips. "Tell me what's wrong, Sunshine."

"I'm nearly twenty-four weeks pregnant."

He places a hand over my belly. "I'm aware."

"But I haven't felt the baby kick yet. I should have felt the baby kick by now. What if there's something wrong with the baby? What if Sprog is in distress? What if—"

He places a finger on my lips. "Hold on. Let's figure this out. Will you let me figure this out?" He raises an eyebrow and I nod.

"First, let's figure out when a pregnant woman should feel a baby kick. We'll go from there."

He digs his phone out of his pocket and scrolls through it. "According to this baby book, you should feel the first kick between the sixteenth and twenty-fourth week."

"Exactly."

"Exactly?" He throws his phone on the bed. "You're not twenty-four weeks yet."

"But Dr. Katz said Sprog is growing faster than normal. If Sprog is growing faster than normal, shouldn't I have felt her kick by now?"

"I don't know. It makes sense, but I'm not a doctor. Let me grab a shower and then I'll drive you to the doctor's office."

My mouth drops open. "You'll drive me to the doctor's office?"

He shrugs. "Yeah. What else do you want to do?"

"This is why I fell in love with you. You're the sweetest grump in the world."

He smiles. "Fell in love?"

My eyes widen when I realize what I said. So much for keeping my mouth shut and not love-vomiting all over him.

"I didn't mean it. It's a turn of phrase is all."

His smile widens and I'm temporarily blinded. Hudson Clark is always handsome, but he's movie star handsome when he smiles.

"I kind of figured out you loved me when you freaked out, I was going to die because all the people you love die."

I groan. "You couldn't have ignored my logic?"

"Nope."

"Can we pretend I didn't say the l-word?"

"Nope."

"I didn't mean to say it."

"Too bad. You did."

"UGH!" I stomp my foot and shout. "Stop being stubborn!"

"I'm not—"

I hold up my hand to quiet him. I place my other hand on my stomach.

"What's wrong? What's happening?" He asks after a few moments of silence.

"I think I felt the baby move. It was a little flutter. The book said making some noise might help but I…" I trail off when I feel another flutter.

He falls to his knees in front of me and cradles my belly. "Hello, Sprog. Your mom and I can't wait to meet you. If you're a girl, you'll be as beautiful as your mom. She's a stunner. And if you're a boy, I'll teach you to play football. Or soccer if you prefer. Or you can take ballet lessons. Whatever you want, you can have."

Tears leak from my eyes as I listen to Hudson speak to our baby. He's going to be the best dad ever. I couldn't help but fall in love with him.

Hold on. I said I love you to Hudson and he basically said, I know. He didn't say it back. Does he not love me? Is this relationship doomed to fail because I love him and he doesn't love me?

I can't be with a man who doesn't love me back. I want the kind of relationship my parents had. I want a man who kisses me goodnight and whispers I love you before wrapping his arms around me and falling asleep together.

But he doesn't love me.

He's going to break my heart.

Chapter 30

Sack – when Hudson gets tackled by an epiphany

HUDSON

I park in front of Weston's apartment building and press the button to call Nova.

"Miss me already?"

I do. The second I left the chalet, I missed her. I rub a hand over my chest where an ache has started. Nova is an addiction and I will happily remain addicted for the rest of my life. No rehab for me in my future.

"Just checking you're okay."

She sighs. "I know I can be a bit over the top with my worries about my health, but you left the house fifteen minutes ago. I'm fine."

"You're not over the top."

"I am, but I appreciate your lie."

"I didn't lie," I grumble.

"Okay, Mr. Cranksville. You didn't lie."

"You don't believe me."

"I believe you believe what you're saying."

I give up. Not for good. But for now. Pushing Nova about her fear of the people she loves dying won't help a thing. She started seeing a therapist and she's giving us a chance. I can't ask any more of her.

"I'll be home in an hour."

She giggles.

"What's funny?"

"You. Thinking you'll be home in an hour."

Weston asked me to help him move some furniture in his apartment. Apparently, he bought a new bedroom set. We'll be done in fifteen minutes and I'll be back on the road.

"I don't understand."

"You've been away from Smuggler's Hideaway too long."

I frown. I wasn't away long enough. I was in the prime of my career when it got cut short by an asshole defensive lineman with an illegal tackle.

"Have fun!" Nova sings before ending the call.

I shove my phone in my pocket and get out of the truck. I climb the stairs to Weston's apartment. His door flies open before I reach it. He grins and throws his arms wide open. "Welcome!"

I grunt. I don't want to be here. I want to be with Nova.

He chuckles as he slaps me on the shoulder and ushers me inside his apartment. I frown when I notice Lucas and Flynn are also here.

"What's going on?"

We don't need four people to move a bit of furniture. If I had known Weston asked Lucas and Flynn to help, I would have said no.

Weston hands me a shot of whiskey. I glare at him. I'm not drinking. I need to be able to drive home. I can't spend a night away from Nova. She's already feeling insecure enough since I haven't told her I love her back.

"I told you this was a bad idea," Flynn says.

What is going on? I study the men before me. Sophia's boyfriend, Flynn. Chloe's husband, Lucas. And Weston. Then, it hits me.

"Is this when you give me the warning to treat Nova right?"

Flynn grins. "You're more than a jock without any brains in his head."

I scowl at him. "Being an athlete doesn't make me stupid."

And I am an athlete. I don't play pro ball anymore, but I will always be an athlete. It's who I am. Who I've always been. Who I always will be.

"No, but messing around with Nova would make you extremely stupid," Weston grumbles.

"Nearly as stupid as the time you decided to triple your protein powder intake in one day and ended up unable to play football because you were too busy racing to the toilet every five minutes," Flynn adds.

I scowl at him. "I hit my growth spurt late."

"You were a freshman and wanted a varsity spot on the high school football team."

Hell, yeah, I did. From the first time I stepped onto a football field, I knew playing the game was my destiny. It's everything I worked for. Everything I wanted. The only thing I care about.

"The wide receiver was crap. I should have had the varsity spot."

"Coach gave you the spot," Flynn says.

"Until you decided to overdose on protein powder," Weston adds.

Lucas chuckles and I growl at him. He holds up his hands. "Sorry, man, but growing up in Smuggler's Hideaway sounds fun."

"It was fun." Weston nudges him. "Natalia is going to love growing up here."

Lucas threads a hand through his hair. "As soon as we get the bully situation dealt with."

Weston frowns. "Natalia is still having problems with Shelia? I thought Chloe dealt with it."

Lucas smiles and the love for his wife is clear to see on his face. "Chloe dealt with the school administration all right. My wife is a force of nature."

"Sophia is too." Flynn narrows his eyes on me. "As is Nova."

"I know she is."

Nova is all smiles and sunshine but she doesn't let anyone push her around. She's amazing.

"Ah." Lucas points to me. "He's in love."

Weston feigns gagging. "Is there something in the water on Smuggler's Hideaway? All my friends are falling in love and pairing up. I guess I better stick to whiskey." He lifts his shot glass. "Cheers."

Flynn and Lucas join him but I set my glass down on the nearest surface. I'm not drinking. I need to be able to drive. Nova is nearly in her third trimester and prone to anxiety about the baby's health. If she wants to go to the hospital, I'm taking her.

"You've given me your warning about treating Nova properly. If there's no furniture to move, I'm out of here."

Weston blocks me before I can make my exit.

"We're not finished yet. I need to make sure your intentions regarding Nova are proper. I'm Nova's honorary big brother."

"As am I," Flynn adds.

Weston wags a finger at him. "No, you're not. She crowned me her honorary big brother when she was ten and I saved her stuffed bunny from the toilet."

"Not to get in between you two, but can't Nova have more than one honorary big brother?" Lucas asks.

I'm done with this shit. I don't have time to waste listening to Flynn and Weston argue about who Nova's honorary big brother is.

"I'm out of here."

"What's your hurry?" Weston asks.

"I need to get home to Nova."

"I heard she's living with you and not moving out when the baby is born," Lucas says.

I cross my arms over my chest. I hate riddles. "If you want to know something, ask me."

"Are you going to kick her out after the baby's born?" Weston asks.

I glare at him. "I would never kick Nova out of her own home."

"Her own home?" He smirks. "She is living with you."

She is. We're at the chalet for now. But she still has her house. I need to speak to her about it. I know she loves the chalet but does she prefer to live at her house? It's the house she grew up in with her parents. She's emotionally attached to it.

But I want to stay in the chalet. It's close to my work. I can be home within minutes to handle any issues that arise with the baby. And the resort has childcare. Plus, we have enough room for a nanny should Nova want one. If she wants to stay home with the baby, that's fine, too.

We still have a lot to figure out. And we will figure it out. Nova loves me. She's in this for the long haul. As am I.

"I don't give a shit where they live," Flynn says. "I want to know if he's going to treat Nova right."

I growl at him. "I will always treat Nova right. She will want for nothing."

Flynn grins. "He has my stamp of approval. He obviously loves Nova."

My brow wrinkles. I obviously love Nova? I admit I'm falling in love with my sunshine. How can I not? She makes everything light and bright.

But love her? I'm not there yet. Love needs years to build.

Weston sighs. "He's a goner for her. I'm going to be the only single man on the island."

Lucas slaps me on the shoulder. "There's no sense fighting it. The women of Smuggler's Hideaway are irresistible."

I don't care about the women of Smuggler's Hideaway. I only care about one woman. Nova.

I don't see any other women. I—

Shit. I do love Nova.

I don't know why I've been fighting it. Love doesn't work with schedules. Love happens. Whether you want it to or not. Whether you're a has-been or not. Whether you ruin good things or not.

Nova is my one good thing I'm not going to ruin. I'm keeping her. And our baby. Forever.

Chapter 31

Treasure hunt – an excuse to drink moonshine and cause havoc

NOVA

I slap my hand on my leg to stop it from bouncing. I'm excited and nervous and impatient. I'm basically a bundle of energy. We're on our way to the doctor's office for the growth scan for baby Sprog. And I can't wait. Maybe this time we'll find out if Sprog is a boy or a girl.

Hudson places his hand over mine.

He doesn't say *don't be nervous* or *everything will be all right*. Words I hate more than a mermaid hates sharks in her water. Trust me. Not everything is all right all of the time.

"We're nearly there."

He turns down the road toward the hospital but has to slam on his brakes before he drives into a group of bikers who are pedaling down the middle of the road. Hudson honks but they don't move.

I roll down my window when I recognize the members of the group.

"What are you doing?" I ask Sophia, Chloe, Maya, and Paisley. "And why wasn't I invited?"

We're the five musketeers, we do everything together. Maya bikes toward the truck but doesn't manage to stop before she slams into the front end. She lands in a heap on the road.

I jump out to help her but Hudson reaches her before me.

"Are you okay? Did you hit your head?" he asks as he helps her to sit.

Sophia, Chloe, Paisley, and I gather around them.

"Wow. You're gorgeous. Not as gorgeous as Caleb but a hottie nonetheless." She pats his cheeks.

"I think you're fine," Hudson says before standing.

"Um, Maya?"

She swivels to glance up at me and nearly falls backward. Hudson steadies her with a hand on her shoulder.

"Hey, Nova. What are you doing here? You shouldn't be drinking. Drinking's bad for the baby."

I giggle. "How much have you had to drink?"

Her nose wrinkles as she counts with her fingers. "One at the start at the *Bootlegger* bar. One at the *Buccaneer's Distillery*. One at the *Mermaid Motel*. And one at the *Rumrunner*."

"You forgot the shot of whiskey at *Mermaid Mini Golf*," Paisley says.

I scan the group. "Why are you out drinking whiskey shots on bikes?"

"The mayor asked us to test out the route for the *Mermaid Treasure Hunt* in two weeks," Sophia says.

The *Mermaid Treasure Hunt* is part of the holiday celebrations on Smuggler's Hideaway. Participants are given a treasure map with clues of where gifts are hidden around the island. Whoever manages to collect the most gifts wins.

And, because this is Smuggler's Hideaway, you have to drink a shot of moonshine every time you find a gift. Which is why the treasure hunt is conducted on bikes.

I raise an eyebrow. "The mayor asked you to test the route?"

"We volunteered!" Chloe squeals.

"Of course, you did."

Paisley frowns at me. "Why the sarcasm? We're the perfect group to test out the route for the *Mermaid Treasure Hunt*."

"We are excellent at figuring out clues," Chloe continues.

"And the loopholes!" Sophia shouts.

It's true. My friends and I are the queens of finding loopholes in contest rules. It's how we won the *Bootlegger Escape Room* weekend festival. I nearly gag at the memory of the hangover I had after the festival. But it was worth it.

I giggle. "In other words, Lana asked you to do the treasure hunt today because she knew you'd figure out how to win at the actual festival in a few weeks."

"We get to be police at the festival," Maya slurs.

"Poor Smuggler's Hideaway," Hudson mutters.

"What do you mean?" Paisley asks. "I will help direct traffic and ensure tourists don't get lost."

"Ha!" Chloe shouts and tips to the side. Sophia helps to prop her up but she's not too steady on her feet either. The two end up slumped together with their arms around each other.

"I'm going to send tourists on a wild goose chase," Chloe continues once she's as steady as it's possible to get after five shots of Smuggler's Hideaway moonshine.

Hudson puts Maya's bike in the back of his truck.

"What are you doing?" I ask when he reaches for Paisley's bike.

"I'm not letting them bike in this condition. I'll call Weston and Lucas and Flynn to pick them up."

My heart warms at the gesture. He's worried about my friends. I know my friends can be a lot, but he's not complaining. He's helping without being asked. Sexy mermaids in the sea, do I love this man.

"No need." Paisley points to the police vehicle pulling to a stop behind Hudson's truck.

"The calvary has arrived!" Chloe shouts before stumbling toward the car. Lucas barely manages to step out of the driver's side in time to catch her before she falls.

He grins down at her. "Are you happy to see me, wildcat?"

"I'm always happy to see you. I love you."

Happiness fills me as I watch my friend gaze up at the man she loves. I never realized how lonely and sad Chloe was until Lucas and Natalia came into her life.

I glance behind me at the man I love. Hudson is staring at the couple with a wrinkled brow. As if he's confused. What is he confused about? Does he not understand how a man could love Chloe? Does he not understand love?

I blow out a breath before panic seizes me. Hudson didn't say he loves me back to me when I confessed my love to him but so what? He obviously cares for me. Doesn't he?

"Do you want me to bring their bikes around later?" Hudson asks Lucas.

"Nah. Flynn is on his way with his truck."

Sophia's nose wrinkles. "Why is Flynn coming to pick up our bikes? I can bike home just fine."

"Except you're sprawled on the road with your legs in the air." I motion to her legs.

"Huh. I wondered why everything was blue." She rolls over and pushes herself into a seating position.

"Sunshine!" Hudson calls.

I smile at him. "What?"

He taps his watch. "We don't want to be late."

"Don't be late for a very important date!" Maya shouts.

"I've got them," Lucas says before herding my friends to the side of the road where they can't jump in front of us – it wouldn't be the first time – and get themselves hurt.

Hudson helps me into the passenger seat of his truck and runs around to the driver's seat.

"Are you in a hurry?"

He shrugs. "I want to find out if we're having a girl or a boy."

"I have an idea."

He blows out a breath. "Please tell me it has nothing to do with the *Mermaid Treasure Hunt*."

I giggle. I have tons of ideas of how to screw with my friends during the treasure hunt but those are for later. "If we find out the gender of the baby, let's not tell anyone."

"You want to keep it a surprise?"

I nod. "We can tell everyone together. Maybe at my baby shower."

"Baby shower?" He curses under his breath. "I knew I was forgetting something. I'll ask my event planner to start working on it."

I roll my eyes. "Terri doesn't need to plan my baby shower. I can do it myself."

We arrive at the hospital and he parks. "Are you sure? I don't want you straining yourself."

"I'm a smuggler. I can plan a party for my friends and family with my eyes closed."

He squeezes my hand. "Promise you'll let me know if it gets to be too much."

"I promise," I whisper before leaning across the console to kiss him.

"My little temptress," he mutters before thrusting his tongue into my mouth. His taste hits me and I scoot closer to him. Except I can't touch him. The stupid console is in the way. I try to climb over it but my belly stops me.

Hudson chuckles before he pulls his lips away from mine. "Appointment." He kisses my nose before exiting the truck and coming around to open my door.

"Maybe you should get a truck without a console in the middle," I complain as he leads me into the hospital.

"I was thinking an SUV."

I blink up at him. "Are you serious?"

He tweaks my nose. "The truck is safe enough but I want a family vehicle for when I drive you and Sprog around."

"As long as it's not a minivan. I am not driving a minivan."

"Duly noted."

He opens the door to Dr. Katz's office and every woman in the place looks over at us. The pregnant women return their attention to their reading but the other women?

Every single one of them tries to catch Hudson's attention. They cross their legs, push out their chests, flutter their lashes. They're sexy and gorgeous. Meanwhile, I'm fat and pregnant and need to pee every five minutes. Not exactly an appealing characteristic.

Hudson helps me into a chair in the corner. "What's wrong?"

I force a smile. "Nothing's wrong."

"Don't lie to me, Sunshine. I can recognize your fake smile."

"I don't have a fake smile."

"It's the same smile you use whenever you have to speak to the sales manager at the Gourmet Corner grocery store."

My nose wrinkles. "He's not a nice man. He told me we need to change all of our packaging despite the CEO saying she loves it."

A nurse enters the waiting room. "Nova Myers."

Hudson scowls as he stands and offers me his hand. "What's wrong? You're not going to bully the sales manager, are you?"

"We'll discuss this later."

I follow the nurse into one of the exam rooms and get changed into one of the gowns. I shiver when Hudson helps me onto the exam table. He frowns.

"Are you cold? We should bring a blanket next time. I don't want you cold."

I pat his cheek. "It's fine. I can handle a bit of cold."

The door flies open and Dr. Katz strolls in. "Ah, look at the two of you. So cute. All loved up."

I don't deny it. I'm totally in love. Hudson isn't, but it's okay. He obviously only has eyes for me. He didn't notice one of the women who was staring at him in the waiting room.

Maybe he just needs time.

"Let's find out if the baby is a girl or a boy."

I focus my attention on the doctor, and Hudson squeezes my hand in support. I gaze up at him, but his gaze is focused on the monitor.

I frown. Is he only being considerate and sweet because of the baby? It's possible. He did ignore me after our night together after all. Until he found out I was pregnant.

Maybe I should slow my roll. Learn how to protect my heart before he breaks it into a million pieces.

Chapter 32

Mean girls – Not limited to cheerleaders who ban you from cheerleading for life

NOVA

"There's no need to be nervous."

I scowl at Hudson. "I'm not nervous."

I'm totally nervous. We're meeting one of Hudson's friends from his time in the NFL. I'd never heard of him before. But I googled Seth Cox and the man is a Big Deal in football. He has four Super Bowl Championship rings, was a Heisman Trophy winner, and is now an assistant coach.

Whereas I sell beer. Of course, I'm nervous.

He places a hand on my knee to stop it from bouncing. "Seth will love you."

I beam at him. "Because I'm awesome."

He chuckles. The sound doesn't surprise me anymore since he's laughing more often but it still causes warmth to spread through my chest whenever he's amused. I love making this man happy. I love him. Plain and simple.

He kisses my forehead. "Yes, you are, Sunshine."

My extremities tingle in excitement. Hudson isn't referring to the baby. He's referring to me. Maybe I don't need to encase my heart behind a concrete wall after all.

My stomach rumbles. "I'm also hungry."

He checks his watch. "Seth is late. Let me give him a call." He reaches for his phone but stops when a giant of a man enters the restaurant. I recognize him from my online search. It's Seth.

Hudson stands with a smile on his face. A real smile. One I haven't seen since we were in high school together. I frown. Is Hudson unhappy living on Smuggler's Hideaway?

Seth holds out his hand and a woman joins him. She is stunning. She's wearing a floor-length sparkly gown. With her long, blonde hair and curvy body, she should be on the front of some glossy fashion magazine.

I glance down at my oversized sweater and plaid, pleated skirt with knee-high black leather boots. I thought I looked cute when I left the chalet but now, I feel fat and frumpy.

As Seth and the woman make their way through the tables to us, every person in the restaurant turns to watch them. The woman tilts her nose into the air and ignores the attention whereas Seth greets the men with claps on the back and high-fives. I fear I underestimated his fame.

"Cox." Hudson greets him with a handshake and back clap.

"Clark. It's been a while. Good to see you, man. You're looking good." He ushers the woman forward. "This is my wife, Naomi."

"Congrats, man. Sorry, I didn't make it to the wedding." Hudson helps me to my feet. "This is my Nova."

Naomi's gaze falls on my belly and her eyes widen. I place my hand over my belly in a protective manner. Sprog can't sense her contempt, but I feel the need to protect him anyway.

Hudson places his arm around my shoulders. "Nova, meet Seth Cox, my former teammate."

I offer him my hand but instead of shaking it, he pulls me into his arms for a hug. Hudson growls and yanks me away from Seth causing his friend to burst into laughter.

"Never thought I'd live to see the day," he says as he pulls out a chair for Naomi. "The great Hudson has fallen for a woman."

Is it true? Has Hudson fallen for me? Am I worried for nothing?

Hudson grunts. Which doesn't enlighten me whatsoever. My insecurity lives to fight for another day.

Seth scans the room. "You're doing well for yourself."

Hudson shrugs, and I hurry to fill the gap. "Hudson owns the entire resort. It's the largest hospitality establishment on the island of Smuggler's Hideaway."

Naomi snorts. "Which isn't saying much."

Is she dissing Smuggler's Hideaway? No one disses the island in my presence. "I grew up here. As did Hudson."

She holds up a hand. "I didn't mean any disrespect."

I force a smile. I know how to deal with mean girls. "None taken. Are you staying on the island?"

"We're here for the weekend," Seth answers. "I heard Clark was here laying low and came to check things out."

"And rehash your glory days," Naomi says.

Seth leans back in his chair and smirks. "I'm still living my glory days."

"What are you doing these days?" Hudson asks.

"Assistant coach of our old team."

"Is the head coach still a ball breaker?"

Seth snorts. "Jerry hasn't changed a damn bit. Do you remember the time he made us run laps in the snow because we were fifteen minutes late to practice?"

"I wasn't fifteen minutes late."

Seth rolls his eyes. "Of course, you weren't." He focuses on me. "This guy is the epitome of discipline. He doesn't shirk from his responsibilities."

"It's better than sneaking out to the bar and getting drunk on tequila shots."

Seth shakes his head. "I still don't remember what happened that night."

"And yet you didn't learn your lesson."

Seth shrugs. "There's more to life than football practice."

Naomi frowns. "There is?"

Seth throws an arm around her chair. "Football is a religion in our family."

Hudson nods in agreement. "Football's a damn good religion to have."

"Do you remember the time you ran for nearly two hundred yards to make a touchdown in overtime? I believed in God then."

I know exactly which game they're referring to. I watched all of Hudson's games when he played. It was hard not to. Smuggler's Hideaway is proud of our football hero.

"I sprained my ankle when I jumped up and down with the ball in the endzone. I spent the next two days icing it while coach yelled at me."

"I didn't realize you sprained your ankle that day," I say.

Hudson grins at me. "Did you watch the game?"

My cheeks heat but I shrug. "Every bar in Smuggler's Rest aired all of your games. It was impossible to avoid."

Seth leans across the table. "Did you watch the time he got tackled and ended up in the lap of the opposing team's coach?"

Naomi stands. "If you two are going to relive your glory days, I'm going to use the powder room."

"I'll go with you," I say.

"There's no need."

I place a hand on my belly. "Sprog makes me have to pee every fifteen minutes."

Hudson helps me to my feet and kisses my cheek. "You, okay?"

I roll my eyes. "I'm fine."

Naomi doesn't wait for me. By the time I catch up to her, she's already in one of the stalls. I try to finish my business as quickly as possible but quick doesn't exactly exist when you're six months pregnant and decided wearing tights was a good idea.

When I exit the stall, Naomi is re-doing her make-up, which appears perfect to me, in front of the mirror.

"I have to say I'm impressed," she says without looking at me.

"Huh?" What is she talking about?

"Snagging the great Hudson Clark."

"He's just Hudson to me. We grew up together here on the island."

She nods to my belly. "Getting pregnant was a good move. It's hard to snag a football legend with your… ahem…assets."

Oh wow. Did she just say I'm ugly? I didn't think Naomi was nice before but it's been confirmed now. She's a mean girl.

"I wasn't trying to snag a football legend."

"It is a shame, though. Hudson is wasting his potential on this Podunk island. He could be a superstar with his looks and playing ability."

"He got injured. He can't play anymore."

She waves a hand at me in dismissal. "He doesn't need to play anymore. He just needs to get back in the game. Get some exposure. The places he could go. But, instead, he's stuck here on this island with you." Her gaze sharpens on my belly.

"I didn't trap him here."

She cocks an eyebrow. "You didn't?"

I didn't trap him. He can leave whenever he wants. I'm not keeping him here. If he wants to leave, he can.

Hold on. Does Hudson want to leave? Does he hate it here? He smiled at Seth in a way I haven't seen him smile since high school. Maybe he does miss football and fame.

I recall the comments he's made about being an athlete. Dang it. Is Hudson miserable and wishing he were still playing football? Is that why he's such a grump?

Naomi finishes applying her lipstick and snaps her purse closed before marching to the door. "Are you coming?"

"Yep."

I smile at her as if my heart isn't breaking. As if I don't have to let Hudson go for him to be happy.

Chapter 33

Realization – Can sometimes hit you harder than a defensive lineman

HUDSON

"Good. The women are gone. We can talk shop," Seth says as soon as Naomi and Nova are out of hearing range.

My brow wrinkles. "Talk shop? You mean reminisce."

"Nope. I mean talk shop."

"There is no shop. My Achilles and ankle are fucked. I can't play anymore."

What I wouldn't give for my words to be a lie. I had at least five more years of playing in the NFL until a defensive player plowed into me with an illegal tackle.

"I saw you running this morning."

"I can run, but I don't have the speed to be a wide receiver anymore."

"You were running pretty fast to me."

I snort. "Everyone appears to run fast to you, slowpoke."

"I'm not a slowpoke."

I cock my brow. "Did you or did you not win the slowest offensive tackle award two years in a row?"

"It's not a real award."

"I remember buying you a damn trophy."

"Because you made up the reward to piss me off."

"I was trying to motivate your ass to go to the gym."

"I went to every practice."

I cross my arms over my chest. "You did the bare minimum. Imagine what you could have done if you had pushed yourself harder with extra workouts."

"Extra workouts didn't help you much."

I flinch.

"Fuck. I'm an asshole," Seth says. "Forget I said anything."

How can I forget how my career was ruined? How I had everything I ever wanted and it was stolen from me in one extremely painful moment.

Seth sighs. "I didn't come here to give you a hard time."

"Nonetheless, you're doing a damn good job."

"I came here to offer you a job."

I shake my head. "I can't play. The doctor said one more bad tackle and I'd never walk again."

"Fuck, man. I don't want to handicap you. I want to use your mind."

I frown. "My mind?"

No one on the football field cares about my mind. They want me to catch the ball and run as fast as possible to outrun the defensive team.

"Coach wants you to be the offensive coordinator."

"Jerry wants me?"

That's difficult to believe. Jerry hasn't contacted me once since I left the team after my injury. Not a call, not a card. Nothing.

"Okay, fine. I want you."

"I'm not interviewing for the offensive coordinator position."

I remember the last time Jerry hired an offensive coordinator. He made those candidates go through five rounds of interviews.

"You don't have to interview."

"Coach never let the offensive coordinator call offensive plays during the game anyway. He insisted on calling all the plays himself."

"Coach has changed."

"Really?" I cock my eyebrow. "You literally said he hasn't changed a bit five minutes ago."

He blows out a breath. "He's still a hard ass, but he recognizes he can't do it all anymore."

"Which is why he's here instead of you."

"He thought you wouldn't want to speak to him."

"Why not?"

"He was kind of a dick to you when you got injured."

Yeah, he was. He pushed me to come back to the team despite what the doctors said. He only let up after the team doctor told him he'd never sign off on my return to the field.

"Anyway." Seth pulls a piece of paper out of his coat jacket and hands it to me. "This is the offer."

"The offer?"

"I told you there's no need for you to interview."

"Jerry signed off on this?"

He nods to the paper I haven't opened. "Yep. And, before you ask, so have the lawyers."

My insides vibrate as excitement rushes through me. This isn't some hare-brained scheme Seth thought up. This is an actual possibility.

I could be back on the field. I miss the smell of the grass, the sound of the gridiron, the roaring of the crowds.

I thought I'd never have it again. I thought I'd ruined the best thing in my life. I thought my time as an athlete was over.

But maybe it's not.

"I'll have Naomi introduce Nova to the other wives. Assuming you want her with you. If not, I'm certain we can figure out visitations. You wouldn't be the first coach to be in this situation."

I growl. 'This situation?' What the hell does he mean? Does he think I knocked Nova up and I'll leave her and our baby behind?

I would never leave Nova or our baby behind. Wherever I go, she's going.

Except Nova would never leave Smuggler's Hideaway. This is her home. Her friends are here. Her business is her. She can't up and move.

And I can't leave Nova. I won't.

I frown. Am I seriously giving up returning to football to stay with Nova? I love her and our baby, but football is my life.

Yet the idea of leaving her – leaving our baby – makes me sick to my stomach. Shit. I can't leave the island. Not even for football.

If I can't leave for the game, maybe football isn't my life after all. Maybe there are other people in my life who are more important than the game.

As exciting as a job as offensive coordinator sounds, it's not for me.

My heart clenches as realization hits me. I'm more than an athlete. I'm not a has-been. I'm a business owner. I'm a father-to-be.

And I'm a Smuggler. Smuggler's Hideaway is home. This is where I belong. Not on the road several months a year with a football team.

Seth holds up his hands. "I didn't mean anything by my comment. I didn't want to assume. After all, you haven't put a ring on it yet."

"I'm waiting."

"For what? She's already knocked up."

"I don't want her to think I'm proposing because of the baby."

His brow wrinkles. "Aren't you?"

"Hell no."

He grins. "Awesome. Happy for you man."

I pass the offer back to him. "I can't accept this."

"You haven't even looked at it."

"I don't need to. My mind's made up." With Nova is where I belong. I choose her. I'm not ruining the best thing I've ever had.

"You could discuss it with Nova. Ask her what she thinks."

I snort. If Nova thinks I want to accept the offer, she'll push me to accept without any regard to her own situation. She'd do anything for me. She's amazing. I don't know why it's taken me this long to admit it to myself. I thought I might love her before but now, I'm sure. She's it. She's the one.

"Promise you'll at least think about it."

I fold the piece of paper and shove it into my back pocket.

"Fine. I'll think about it." I notice Nova making her way to our table. "Let's discuss this later."

When she arrives, I notice her face is pinched. "Are you okay? Are you feeling queasy? Do you want to leave and I'll make you some of my chicken noodle soup?"

She smiles at me but it doesn't light up her face. "I'm okay. I want to stay and get to know your friend better."

I scan her face for any sign she's in distress. "Fine. But if you start feeling nauseous, you have to let me know."

She rolls her eyes. "I promise, Grumpalotoulos."

"Still not Greek," I mutter as I pull out her chair for her and help to situate her.

"Still a grump," she sings back to me.

I chuckle as I sit next to her.

This is why I won't accept the job. I don't want to miss these moments. And I know how these moments can stack up.

When I returned to the island three years ago, my brothers weren't snotty-nosed kids anymore. They were young men. I missed those years with them.

I'm not missing any moments with Nova. Or Sprog. I will be there for every milestone Sprog experiences. Side by side with the woman I love.

Chapter 34

Laundry – a dangerous task that should be avoided at all cost

NOVA

I force myself out of bed. When Hudson got up to go for a run, I rolled over and went back to sleep. It's Sunday. Doesn't he understand Sundays are for sleeping in? Drinking coffee in bed and generally being lazy.

I'm going to enjoy being lazy for a little while longer. As soon as Sprog arrives, lazy days will be over. I can't wait.

Speaking of Sprog, I need to pee. Again.

When I finish in the bathroom, Hudson still isn't back from his run. Welp. I'm awake now. I might as well get a load of laundry started. Hudson wants me to send our laundry to the resort laundromat, but I would never take advantage of his position as the owner. I can do laundry.

I'm checking all the pockets are empty before I throw the clothes into the washing machine when I feel a crinkle from the back pocket of Hudson's jeans. I pull out the paper and set it on the washing machine before getting the rest of the load ready.

I switch on the machine and grab the piece of paper intent on putting it on his desk in his office. I'm not going to read it. It's none of my business.

I set the paper on Hudson's desk and start toward the hallway. But I can't stop staring at the piece of paper. What is it?

It's probably just some boring work thing he forgot was in his pocket. But there was nothing in his pocket when we walked to the restaurant last night to meet Seth. I know since I couldn't keep my hands off of him. It was his fault. He's the one who kissed me. I can't help it if his ass is too sexy to not touch.

It has to be something Seth brought him. But what would his former teammate bring him?

The curiosity is killing me.

"Fine! I'll look!"

I march to the paper and unfold it. *Offer. Offensive Coordinator. Starting salary. Bonuses.*

I collapse on the office chair. Hudson was offered the position of offensive coordinator for his old team for an obscene amount of money and he didn't tell me.

There's only one reason he wouldn't tell me. He's going to accept the position.

He's leaving me and Sprog.

I knew this would happen! I knew he would break my heart!

Naomi was right. I'm a nobody from Nowheresville and Hudson is a star who should shine bright. He shouldn't be stuck here with me because I'm pregnant. I need to let him go.

I march to the bedroom. I can pack and be out of here in no time. There's no reason to prolong the pain. Ripping the bandage off is better.

"Hey," Hudson greets as he walks toward me in the hallway. I was in such a tizzy I didn't hear him come home.

"I'll be out of your hair in fifteen minutes."

"What?"

"You're right. Fifteen minutes is too little. Thirty minutes."

"What the hell are you talking about?"

"Okay, fine. More like an hour. I'll message my friends. If they come, I'll be faster."

Hudson shackles my wrist as I try to pass him. "You're not making any sense, Nova."

"I'm not making sense! I'm not the one who's keeping secrets!" I tug on his hold but he doesn't release me.

"You need to slow down. Stress isn't good for the baby."

I push up on my tiptoes to get in his face. "All you care about is the baby. You don't care about me."

"What are you talking about? I care about you."

"Because I'm growing your baby inside of me. But don't you worry. Me and the baby will be out of your hair momentarily." I tug on his hold again. "As soon as you let me go."

"I'm not letting you go," he growls. "I'm never letting you go."

"Really?" I throw my free arm in the air. "How is that going to work when you're off galivanting with the team while I'm here on Smuggler's Hideaway being a boring mom and beer salesperson?"

"Galivanting?"

"It means—"

"I know what it means," he says and cuts me off. "What I don't know is why you're talking about me off galivanting."

"I saw," I seethe.

"Saw what?"

This time when I yank on his hold, it works and I manage to retreat a few steps from him. "You're leaving me."

"You have to help me out here."

"Help you? You want *me* to help *you* get a job that earns one million dollars a year? Are you out of your mind?"

"Shit," he swears under his breath.

"Now you get it. And I need to leave."

He blocks my departure. "You are not going anywhere."

"I'll go wherever I want."

"I'm not going anywhere either."

"Of course not. This is your chalet."

"Listen to me, Sunshine. I am not going anywhere. I'm not leaving. I'm not accepting the job."

"Why not? Isn't offensive coordinator your perfect job?"

"I thought it was."

My heart seizes. I was right. He's leaving me.

"Sunshine." He cradles my face with his hands. "Hear me. I *thought* it was. I was wrong. Football is my past."

"But you always sound full of regret whenever I bring up your football career."

He cringes.

"Exactly. Like that!"

He blows out a breath. "Can we sit down?" He doesn't wait for my answer before picking me up and carrying me to the bedroom.

"You can't carry me around without my permission."

He lays on the bed and settles me on top of him so I'm straddling him.

"I'm sorry. I shouldn't have carried you without your permission but you were swaying and it scared me."

"Oh."

"Can I speak now?"

I shrug. "You can speak, but it won't change a thing."

"Sunshine, what I have to say changes everything."

A tiny spark of hope ignites in my belly. I try to extinguish it. Having my hopes crushed will make things hurt even worse than they already do.

"I did regret the end of my football career. I thought being an athlete is who I am. But when Seth offered me the position, I realized an athlete is not *who* I am, it's *what* I was. There's more to me than my ability to catch a ball or sprint down a football field."

"Of course, there is. You're the owner of this resort. A resort everyone on the island thought was doomed to fail."

His brow wrinkles. "The smugglers thought I was doomed to fail?"

"Have you seen the price of your rooms? And the chalets cost even more. Most tourists to Smuggler's Hideaway stay in the *Mermaid Hotel* and go to the *Rumrunner* for two-dollar beer night. Your hoity-toity resort wasn't a step up. It was another floor all together."

"The smugglers thought I was going to fail," he mutters.

"But you didn't." I clear my throat. "There's clearly more to you than football. There always has been. You practically raised your brothers. You're a great son. All of your employees rave about your management skills."

"They do?"

I frown at him. "Don't beg for compliments. It's unbecoming."

"I wasn't begging for compliments."

"But if you want to accept this position, I'm not going to stand in your way. Which is why I need to leave."

My hands tremble and my eyes are itchy but I'm not standing in his way. If this is what Hudson needs to be happy, I'll make sure he gets it. All I want is for him to be happy. Even if it's not with me.

I start to climb off of his lap but he clamps his hands on my hips to stop me.

"I'm trying to tell you I don't want the position, Sunshine. I don't want to leave you or Sprog. I love you."

My mouth drops open. "What?"

He uses a finger to close my mouth. "I love you. I think I've known it for a while, but I was afraid."

"Afraid of what? I'm not scary. Besides the one time with the high school principal but really, she should have known not to enter the office when the door wasn't locked."

He chuckles. "I have no idea what you're talking about, my crazy girl. But I wasn't scared of you. I was scared I'd ruin us. I'm good at ruining good things."

"What good things have you ruined? If you say your football career, I'm going to throat punch you."

He barks out a laugh. "You're going to throat punch me? I tell you I love you and this is your response?"

"I love you, too, but you know this. What you don't seem to know is that you don't ruin good things and you're more than your football career. Someone has to set you straight."

"And you're the person who's going to do it."

I shrug. "I think I signed up for the position when I fell in love with you."

He draws his hands up my sides, skimming along my breasts, until he reaches my neck. "I love you, Nova. I don't deserve you. I'm a grump and you're sunshine, but I'm not letting you go."

I wrinkle my nose. "You're not always a grump." He smiles and I point at his face. "You smiled. Thanks for proving my point."

"I can't wait to spend the rest of my life with you."

I smile. "Same."

"There she is, my sunshine."

He uses his hold on my neck to pull me close and molds his lips to mine. I moan and he thrusts his tongue into my mouth. I love how he kisses me as if he can never get enough. As if he loves the taste of me.

I understand since I love the taste of him, too. I love being surrounded by his sandalwood scent and feeling his warmth against my body. His hard muscles against my soft curves.

He pulls back and places his forehead against mine. "What do you say to a shower together?"

"I'll never say no to a joint shower."

He lifts me off of his lap. "Just try not to drown me this time."

"I make no promises," I sing as I rush into the bathroom. He chases after me.

I hope he always chases after me.

Chapter 35

Baby shower – an excuse for Hudson to spoil his sunshine

NOVA

I bustle around the kitchen checking to make sure everything is ready. I want everything to be perfect for the baby shower. I can't wait to surprise my friends with the gender of the baby.

"Sunshine," Hudson growls.

"I'll sit down in a minute."

He's been growling at me to sit down every few seconds. He acts as if I'm made of glass since I'm pregnant. As if women haven't been having babies since the beginning of time.

He grasps my elbow and guides me toward a chair. "You're nearly eight months pregnant."

The past months have flown by since Hudson declared his love. Christmas was the best holiday I've had since Mom was alive. I missed her something terrible but Hudson was there to hold me when it got too much. And his mom, Emma, is an absolute saint who is beyond excited to become a grandmother.

I place a hand over my belly. "I'm aware."

"You should rest. You don't need—"

"Shhh…" I shush him and grab his hand. I place it on my belly. "Did you feel Sprog?"

The baby kicks again and Hudson's eyes light up. "Sprog is one strong baby."

"Because Sprog's daddy is the strongest man I know."

He smiles and my heart warms at the sight. Hudson is no longer the grumpiest man in the world, but his smiles are still rare and therefore precious to me. He's precious to me.

"I have a surprise for you."

I roll my eyes. "No more surprises. You have to stop spoiling me."

He helps me to my feet. "I love you. I'll spoil you as much as I want."

"What if I become a spoiled brat?"

He barks out a laugh. "My sunshine will never be a spoiled brat."

"I don't know. Maybe I expect you to buy me a new car every Christmas from now on."

Yes, a car. Hudson doesn't do small Christmas gifts.

"You yelled at me in front of my entire family for buying you a car."

I shrug. "So, what if I did?"

He tweaks my nose. "You will never be a spoiled brat."

He leads me to the sliding doors to the back patio. "Is the construction on the patio done?"

There was a problem with the support beams for the deck. Workmen have been making a racket for a week now.

"Yes! I was hoping they would finish before the baby shower."

He pulls the drapes open. "It's done."

"Great. We can…" My voice trails off when I realize there's more than a repaired deck back here. There's an entire swimming pool. "You put in a pool?"

I yank on the sliding glass doors to open them but they don't move. Hudson nudges me out of the way before sliding the door open and ushering me outside.

"What do you think?"

"I think you didn't need to build me a pool. I already agreed to put my house on the market and live with you."

"And this is me thanking you. I know how much that house meant to you."

"Not as much as you do."

He kisses my nose. "Love you, Sunshine. Now what do you think of your new pool?"

I hesitate for a second before giving in and hurrying to the edge of the pool. "It's gorgeous! I love swimming pools!"

"I know."

"I can't wait to swim in it when the weather gets a bit warmer."

"You can swim in it now. It's heated."

I gasp. "Heated?" I toe off my shoe and dip my foot in the water. The warm water. "What time is it? When are the guests coming? Do I have time for a quick swim?"

He laughs as he helps me put my shoe back on. "The guests will be here any minute. You can go for a swim after the party. If you're awake."

I slap his shoulder. "No making fun of the pregnant woman for needing her sleep."

"I wouldn't dare." He leads me back inside. Just as the doorbell rings to indicate our first guests have arrived. I go to open the door with Hudson hot on my heels.

"Welcome!" I greet Weston.

He scowls. "I don't know why men have to attend a baby shower."

"Be nice," a woman scolds him.

He sighs before wrapping an arm around her and grinning down at her. "Nova, this is my Scarlett."

I rub my eyes. "I must be seeing things. Weston Milton with a woman?"

"That's what I said," Scarlett quips.

I smile at her. "We're going to be great friends."

"Congratulations." She places a gift in my hands. "I hope you like it. I didn't know what to get you since we haven't met yet."

"Blame him." I point at Hudson. "He doesn't want me going to Drunk Poker unless he drives me. Apparently, being pregnant affects your ability to drive. But he did buy me a new car for Christmas."

"I'm confused. He bought you a new car but he doesn't want you to drive?"

"Exactly! He makes no sense."

Hudson kisses my hair. "I'm getting a drink with Weston."

Weston squeezes Scarlett's hand. "Are you okay?"

"I'm fine. Go have a drink. I'll drive home."

He scowls. "You are not driving home. I'll have one drink and switch to water." He kisses her cheek before following Hudson to the wet bar.

"Wait!" I rush after him with the tray of ribbons. "You have to choose sides."

He stares at the blue and pink ribbons in confusion.

"Blue for a boy. Pink for a girl."

"You're revealing the gender?" He rubs his hands together. "What do I get when I guess correctly?"

"Everyone goes home with a goodie bag." He frowns. "But the goodie bag for the winners is better."

"How much better?" He glances around. "Where are these goodie bags?"

Scarlett elbows him. "I swear he isn't always a jerk."

"I'm never a jerk to you." He waggles his eyebrows at her and she giggles.

I shake my head. "The mighty Weston has fallen. I wouldn't have believed it if I didn't see it for myself."

"See what for yourself?" Sophia asks as she enters with Flynn.

I point to Weston. "Your brother in love."

"It's awesome. I finally have a sister."

I scowl at her. "I'm your sister."

She grins at me. "And I'm going to be the best auntie your baby could ever have."

"You can be the best aunt. I'll be the best uncle," Brooks says as he strolls inside the chalet with his brothers trailing behind him.

I sigh. "You're going to cause our baby to get into so much trouble."

"It'll be awesome." He winks.

I hold up the tray. "Pick your poison. Pink if you think the baby, is a girl. Blue if you think the baby, is a boy."

Brooks grabs two blue ribbons.

"What are you doing? I'm only having one baby."

He puts one ribbon back. "Just checking."

"Ha!" Sawyer holds out his hand. "You owe me money."

Hudson growls at his brothers. "You better not be betting on our baby."

"They're betting on whether you're carrying twins and whether the baby is a girl or a boy," Logan says.

Owen glares at him. "Tattletale."

"Don't make fun of your brother," Emma says as she joins us with Hudson's dad.

I glance around and notice the chalet has completely filled up with our friends and family. I wave to Maya who's standing by herself in the corner. She's not good with crowds even if she knows most of the people in attendance.

"Listen up!" Hudson hollers. "We'll be revealing Sprog's gender today. Pick a blue ribbon for a boy or a pink ribbon for a girl. Pick one ribbon only." He glares at his brothers. "There is only one baby."

I walk through the crowd ensuring everyone has a chance to pick a ribbon. Once everyone has one, I return to Hudson.

"We're going outside for the reveal," Hudson announces before ushering everyone outside onto the new patio.

"Awesome!" Owen shouts when he sees the pool. "We're going to have epic pool parties here."

Hudson wraps an arm around my shoulders and leans in to whisper in my ear, "Don't worry. I already have contractors on the ready to build a pool at my parents' house."

"Your brothers are welcome to swim here."

"My brothers are hellions."

I point to where Brooks is stripping off his clothes. "I kind of figured."

Hudson shakes his head before leading me to the board filled with balloons. I had planned to do the reveal inside but since the construction on the deck is done, we can do this outside.

I glance around at our guests. "I don't think giving our guests darts is such a great idea."

He kisses my hair. "Don't worry. I won't let anyone harm you."

I'm not worried about me. I'm worried Smuggler's Hideaway emergency services can't handle fifty people needing stitches all at the same time.

Hudson picks up the tray of darts before explaining how the gender reveal works. "Everyone gets one chance to hit a balloon. One balloon reveals Sprog's gender but which one?"

"Me first." Chloe rushes to the front of the line and throws her dart. Water splashes out of the balloon but no color. "I want to go again."

Sophia shoves her out of the way. "My turn." Her balloon doesn't have any color either.

Paisley pushes her glasses up her nose as she studies the board. She takes aim and hits a balloon on the bottom row. It bursts and the color pink explodes.

Maya rushes to me and throws her arms around me. "A girl. You're having a girl. I'm so happy for you."

I wipe the tears from my eyes. "I always wanted a little girl."

"I'm going to spoil your daughter rotten."

"You need to get in line." I thumb my finger at Hudson. "Daddy is going to spoil his little girl rotten."

Hudson frowns as he marches to me. "Why are you crying?"

"Because I'm happy."

He wipes away the tears. "I don't want you to cry."

"Too bad I'll cry if—

"Cannonball!" Brooks shouts and I glance over in time to watch him jump into the pool. He splashes several guests who laugh and begin stripping.

"Fuck," Hudson mutters. "I'll get him."

"Let him be. He's having fun. It's a party."

"It's supposed to be your baby shower."

"It still is. We revealed Sprog's a girl. I got tons of presents. And everyone's having a good time. The baby shower is a success."

I spot someone standing to the side of the chalet.

"Is that Caleb?"

Hudson nods.

"What is he doing here?"

"He lives in one of the chalets on the edge of the property. I couldn't not invite him."

"Lives in one of the chalets? Caleb is stationed overseas."

Hudson shrugs. "I guess he's back home."

"But he didn't tell anyone."

"I didn't know it was a secret."

"I need to find Maya." I scan the crowd but I don't see her. "She should be warned he's home."

Hudson motions to Maya marching toward Caleb. "You're too late."

I start toward her but he shackles my wrist. "Let them work it out for themselves."

"You're home!" Maya shouts and throws herself at him.

He catches her but sets her on her feet before stepping back. "I knew I shouldn't have come to this party." He marches away. Maya chases after him.

"I should…"

"Let them be. And enjoy your party." Hudson motions to the pool where his brothers are now playing a rigorous game of volleyball against my friends.

I sigh. "I love the family we've created."

He places a hand over my belly. "I love our little family."

I smile up at him and he kisses me. My lips tingle and my belly warms. This man can get me excited with a simple kiss. I hope he always can.

Because I'm never giving him up. I tried once. It didn't take.

Chapter 36

Maya – a woman who's about to get the surprise of her life

MAYA

I frown when I notice how crowded Nova and Hudson's chalet is. Paisley pats my shoulder.

"Don't be afraid. Pretend this is one of your romance novels."

If she only knew. I always pretend my life is a romance novel. It's the only way I can manage to enter rooms with large groups of people.

"Thanks."

"Always. I'm always here for you."

She is. I have a great group of friends. But Sophia and Chloe aren't around as much anymore since they've found love. And now Nova is all loved up, too.

Soon I'll be all alone again. Paisley will probably fall in love before me, too. It's kind of hard to fall in love when you've been obsessed with a boy you went to high school with for most of your life.

A boy who's now a man in the military and is always stationed overseas. Mostly in really scary places he won't tell me about. A man who is merely my pen pal buddy. And will never be more.

Paisley herds me toward the bar. "Let's get a drink."

I drag my feet. "I'm driving."

"This is Nova's baby shower. I'm certain she has non-alcoholic drinks."

Drat. There goes my excuse for staying on the edge of the crowd.

Pretend this is a romance novel. I imagine I'm the youngest daughter of a duke being forced to go to a ball against her will. Her father is ready for her to marry but she's in love with the gardener. He's forbidden since he's a commoner.

By the time Paisley shoves a non-alcoholic beer in my hand, I'm warming up to my story. I bet the gardener is sexy. I imagine he's over six-foot tall and has bulging muscles. I add blond hair and blue eyes to the image. Maybe a cute dimple to soften his face.

Paisley hands me a pink ribbon and brings me out of my fantasy. "What's this?"

"Nova and Hudson are doing a gender reveal. Guests are supposed to pick a pink or blue ribbon based on what gender they think the baby is." She waves her blue ribbon. "There were only two left."

"The baby is going to be a girl. I know it."

"Which is why I gave you the pink ribbon. Come on. The reveal is happening outside."

I hurry to follow Paisley out the back doors. There are just as many people outside, but it doesn't feel as scary when there are no walls barreling down on me.

Paisley leads me to where Chloe and Sophia are standing. I scan the area for Chloe's stepdaughter. "Where's Natalia?"

Chloe points to the pool. "She's over there."

"When did Nova get a pool?" Paisley asks.

"Hudson had it built for her as a present for her baby shower," Sophia says. "You know how she hates to swim in the ocean."

Chloe giggles. "I accept full credit. Nova has some kick on her. She nearly broke my nose."

"You shouldn't have scared her by tugging on her leg," I say.

Paisley frowns. "Why she was convinced a shark was trying to drown her is a mystery to me. Sharks don't have hands."

"She panicked. No one thinks rationally when they panic."

"Which explains why you ran out of biology class shouting 'the English are coming' when you were supposed to give your presentation," Sophia says.

"I don't understand why we had to give a presentation anyway. It was biology class," I mutter.

"Public speaking is a valuable skill," Paisley says.

I snort. "You fall asleep whenever I start to talk about the quarterly numbers."

"Numbers are boring," Chloe declares.

Not to me they aren't. They're reliable and dependable. And, best of all, I don't need to speak to anyone when it comes to my job as the financial manager for *Five Fathoms Brewing*. Except for those pesky clients who refuse to pay. Lucky for me, an email will often suffice.

Numbers aren't exciting like romance, though. If I could write romance books, I'd be a writer and spend my days in my head dreaming of ways for the hero and heroine to fall in love. But one creative writing class in college taught me I have no writing skills whatsoever. So, numbers it is.

Chloe claps her hands. "It's time for the gender reveal. I'm totally popping the balloon with the color."

She pushes her way through the crowd until she's in the front. "Me first."

She throws her dart at the board filled with balloons. Water splashes out of the balloon she hit but there's no color. She scowls. "I want to go again."

Sophia shoves her out of the way. "My turn."

Chloe stomps back to us. "No fair. I'm sure I would have gotten it right with my second balloon."

I giggle. "You were the one who insisted on going first."

Sophia throws her dart, but her balloon doesn't have any color either.

"I believe I have this figured out." Paisley pushes her glasses up her nose before marching to the front. She picks up a dart, takes aim, and hits a balloon on the bottom row. It bursts and the color pink explodes.

"I knew it!" I shout before rushing to Nova and throwing my arms around her. "A girl. You're having a girl. I'm so happy for you."

I step back and she wipes tears from her eyes. "I've always wanted a little girl."

I know she has. I'm so happy for her I'm about to burst. Nova is living her own romance novel. She deserves it after losing her parents at such a young age. She deserves all the good things.

"I'm going to spoil your daughter rotten."

"You need to get in line." She thumbs her finger at Hudson. "Daddy is going to spoil his little girl rotten."

Hudson frowns as he marches to us. "Why are you crying?"

The tender way he gazes at Nova has my stomach cramping with envy. I sneak away. I don't want to ruin their moment with my jealousy. I want my friend to have everything she's ever wanted. Including the grumpy resort owner she claimed to hate. I knew she didn't hate him.

One of Hudson's brothers – I can't tell them apart yet – jumps into the pool and several people join them, including my friends. I don't have my swimsuit on and unlike the other people here, I'm not swimming in my bra and panties.

I find a quiet area to watch the party from. I'm not miserable. I enjoy observing other people have fun.

I'll make sure to remember it all and then write it in my next letter to Caleb. I frown. I haven't heard from him in a while. He doesn't write as often as I do but usually, I receive at least one letter a month. But I haven't gotten a letter this month.

Speaking of Caleb, the man leaning against the corner of the chalet could be his twin. Same height. Same bulging muscles. Same blond hair. Same blue eyes.

Hold on a minute. It is Caleb.

"Caleb! You're home!" I shout as I run his way and throw myself at him.

He catches me but immediately sets me back on my feet before retreating. "I knew I shouldn't have come to this party." He turns around and marches away without another word.

What? Why is he being a meanie? I chase after him.

"Caleb. It's me, Maya. Your pen pal," I explain as I try to keep up. He's limping but despite the limp, he's moving way faster than me. "Slow down."

"Fuck," he mutters before stopping.

"Why are you limping? Are you injured? Is that why you're home? When did you get home? Why didn't you tell me?"

"I didn't tell you because I didn't want to see you."

My eyes widen. "What? Why not?"

"It's not personal."

"Feels pretty personal when you tell me you don't want to see me after twelve years of being pen pals."

He rubs the top of his head. "I meant I don't want to see anyone."

"Not anyone? What about your family? They've missed you."

He scowls. "My family is better off without me."

"What are you talking about? They're your family. They aren't better off without you. They love you."

Unlike my family members who were happy to see the backside of me. We don't speak. I send birthday cards and Christmas cards but I never receive anything in return. I can't remember the last time my mother phoned for my birthday.

And I'm not invited to Christmas dinner. Traitors aren't welcome.

"You're better off without me, too."

Pain crashes through my chest at his words. Better off without Caleb? Never. Caleb is everything.

"How about I choose whether I'm better off without you? It's this new thing I'm trying out. Being an adult woman and making my own decisions. It agrees with me thus far."

He ducks his head but not before I notice his lips turn up in a barely-there smile.

"I'm trying to protect you here."

"Protect me from what? Spending time in real life with the person I've been writing letters to for over a decade?" I narrow my eyes on him. "Or did you ask someone else to write those letters? Have you been pretending to be someone else? Let me guess. You're a super secret spy who's here on a mission because the island has been invaded by aliens."

"Aliens?" He barks out a laugh. "My shy Maya is funny."

"Funny and shy aren't mutually exclusive."

He shakes his head. "Apparently not."

"Come on. Let's go back to the party. Rumor has it they have beer from *Five Fathoms Brewing*, which I have to tell you is the best beer on the island. Not only on the island but in the US. Maybe in the world. I tried to send some to you but it's prohibited to send alcoholic beverages to soldiers fighting in Afghanistan, which I learned when some Army dude showed up on my doorstep to ask me if I worked for a terrorist organization."

He scowls. "Who came to your door? Did they scare you?"

"I nearly peed my pants when he asked me if I agree with Americans being beheaded." I shiver. "Of course, I don't. I don't think anyone should be beheaded. I don't even agree with the death penalty. I know you do. Let's not argue about it now."

"I'll find out who it is and speak to them."

I roll my eyes. "No need to go Rambo on him. He left pretty quick after he noticed all the romance books in my house. He seemed kind of scared."

"You're still obsessed with romance novels?"

"I wouldn't say obsessed. More like enamored."

"Maya!" Paisley shouts. I glance over my shoulder. All of my friends are standing near the chalet watching us.

"I need to go," Caleb says. "Stay safe, Maya."

"That sounds like goodbye!" I shout after him.

"Because it is!"

Silly man. As if he can get rid of me that easily. I now have a mission. Find out why Caleb thinks everyone in his life is better off without him. And then convince him he's wrong.

Chapter 37

Introducing Iliana

TWO MONTHS LATER

Hudson

I glare at Nova. "We're going to the hospital."

She grits her teeth as she fights another wave of pain. I can't stand watching her in pain. I need to do something about it. Which is go to the hospital.

"It's not time yet."

"You're in pain. Whenever you're in pain, it's time to go to the hospital."

"No, it's not, Crabby Crabapple."

Any man would be crabby after watching the woman they love suffer through pain for several hours.

"You're having our baby. I don't want you to give birth to our baby girl in this chalet."

"Why not? Women give birth at home all the time."

I blow out a breath before I snap at her. Me yelling will not get us to the hospital any quicker. I kneel in front of her and grasp her hands.

"You're not being a hypochondriac if you go to the hospital when you're having contractions."

"It's early labor. I don't need to go to the hospital until my contractions last at least one minute each and occur at least every five minutes for more than two hours."

This is what I get for buying every single book about pregnancy I could find. Nova memorized everything she could about labor. She's determined to overcome her hypochondria. Considering Dr. Katz rang up last week to ask if everything is okay since she hadn't heard from Nova in over a week, she's winning the battle.

"Sunshine, no one will think you're a hypochondriac if you go to the hospital now."

She scowls at me.

"I'm so fucking proud of you. You've worked really hard to fight your fear of death. I'm in awe of your strength."

Tears well in her eyes and she sniffs to stop them from falling but one manages to escape. I wipe it away.

"I'm serious, Sunshine. You're the strongest person I know."

"Thank you and I love you, but I'm not going to the hospital until my contractions occur every five minutes for two hours."

"Can we compromise?"

She giggles. "Listen to you. Captain Cranky is going to compromise."

"I compromise with you all the time. Didn't I let you go out with your friends last week despite worrying about how close you are to your due date?"

She rolls her eyes. "You gave me a curfew."

I shrug. "It was either a curfew or I was going with you."

"It's hard to gossip about our men when one of the men is with us."

"Which is why I compromised. And now it's time for another compromise."

She sighs. "There are rules about when a woman should go to the hospital for labor. There isn't room for compromise."

"But you're in pain."

"And I'm a woman. I can handle it."

"What do you want? Say the word and you can have it. If you agree to go to the hospital now."

She smiles and despite the pain obvious to see in her eyes, it lights up her face. "I have everything I want. I have the man I love kneeling in front of me. And we're having a baby together. What else could I possibly want for in life?"

Damn. She makes a good argument, but I'm not giving up this easily.

"How about a hot tub? We can add it next to the swimming pool. Think about it. We could go out there and relax in the hot water, no matter the weather. In fact, our deck is completely isolated. We could go naked."

She wags her finger at me. "You've been trying to get me to skinny dip since the day you installed the pool."

I waggle my eyebrows. "And you promised you would skinny dip when you're not pregnant."

"And I've lost the baby fat."

"What do you say?" I push. "I can have the hot tub installed tomorrow."

"You don't need to buy me things."

"I enjoy buying you things. It makes me happy."

"And I enjoy making you happy."

"Then, accept the hot tub and make me happy by agreeing to go to the hospital."

"I don't need a hot tub."

I frown. "What about if I have a beer tap installed in our bar? We could stock whatever *Five Fathoms* beer you want."

"We already have all the *Five Fathoms* beer I want."

"What about—"

"Enough!" She holds up her hand. "I don't want anything material from you. All I want is you."

"I'm trying to compromise here."

She frowns.

"What is it? Another contraction? Let me time it." I grab my phone to start the timer.

"There's no need."

"Not a contraction?"

"I mean there's no need to compromise anymore." She cringes. "My water broke. It's a good thing I put a towel down on this chair."

"I don't give a fuck about the chair." I lift her in my arms and begin to carry her to the door.

She bats my shoulders. "Wrong way. I need to change my clothes first."

"Fuck your clothes. We have a bunch of clean clothes in your go bag."

"I am not going to the hospital with soaked panties."

"Yes, you are."

"Hudson Clark, turn your rearend around and carry me to the bedroom to change my clothes this minute or I won't give you a blow job until this baby is in college."

Damn. She's serious. I whirl around and head toward the bedroom.

Once she's changed into clean, dry clothes, I carry her to my truck and drive her to the hospital. We arrive and I stop in front of the emergency room. I jump out and run to the passenger door.

"What are you doing? You're blocking the emergency room door."

"Nova, you are an emergency," I say as I pick her up and carry her toward the entrance.

"Promise you'll move the truck once I'm inside."

"I promise." I'd promise her anything right now.

I set her in a wheelchair and push her toward the reception desk. Dr. Katz is waiting for us there.

"It's about time you got here," she greets.

Nova's brow wrinkles. "I only called you five minutes ago."

Dr. Katz points to me. "The big guy rang me this morning when you had your first contraction."

Nova twists to glare up at me. "I told you not to bother the doctor."

The doctor laughs. "Follow me. I've got your room ready."

I walk with the doctor as we head to the maternity ward. I roll Nova into the room and help her get situated on the bed.

She glances around. "There's only one bed in here."

"Because Daddy wanted a private room," Dr. Katz answers.

Nova frowns at me. "I don't need a private room."

"Maybe I need a private room." I kiss her nose. "There's a couch in here I can sleep on until you and little Sprog can come home."

"Dang it. How am I supposed to stay mad at you when you do such sweet things?"

I grin. "You're not supposed to be mad at me when you're having my baby."

"On the contrary, I'm pretty certain I get to be mad at you and scream all kinds of obscenities at you when the pain gets to be too much."

"Which is why you're having an epidural."

"Let me have a look." The doctor sits on the stool between Nova's legs. "It might be too late for an epidural. Yep," she says a moment later. "Baby Myers is on her way. No time for an epidural."

"Baby Clark."

She clears her throat. "My apologies. Baby Clark."

Despite Dr. Katz's announcement about the baby being born soon, it's another three hours before our baby girl arrives in the world.

When the nurse finally places the baby on Nova's chest, Nova sighs as she runs her finger down the little, tiny nose. "You're perfect, Iliana."

"Iliana?" I ask. "I thought we'd name the baby after your mother."

"Her middle name will be Stella. Iliana Stella Clark."

Love for this tiny creature fills me. "I love you, Iliana."

Tears run down Nova's face. "I have everything I've ever wanted."

I wipe her tears away and kiss her forehead. "Thank you for giving me the world. I love you, Nova."

She smiles at me and warmth fills me. "I love you, too, Hudson."

I never thought giving into the temptation that is Nova Myers would lead me to love and family, but it has. I don't need football to be happy. This is what true happiness is.

There's only one thing I have left to do. Convince Nova to marry me.

D.E. Haggerty

Love and Laughter in Every Chapter

About the author

D.E. Haggerty is an American who has spent the majority of her adult life abroad. She has lived in Istanbul, various places throughout Germany, and currently finds herself in The Hague. She has been a military policewoman, a lawyer, a B&B owner/operator and now a writer.

Printed in Great Britain
by Amazon